TOBY TYLER

This is the classic story of a small boy who, like many other small boys, dreamed of running away and joining a circus. Only, Toby Tyler really did it! Uncle Dan'l at home didn't seem to think much of Toby, so he listened to the persuasive words of a circus man who told him what a wonderful adventure he would have.

It didn't take poor Toby long to find out how wrong he had been. If it hadn't been for the sympathetic monkey, Mr. Stubbs, and the kindhearted Fat Lady and her husband, the Skeleton, and little Ella, the bareback rider, Toby would have been miserable indeed. But he did learn a great lesson, and the story of his adventures has delighted four generations of children.

*It really seemed as if the monkey was pleased to know
that his little friend was not hurt*

TOBY TYLER

OR

Ten Weeks with a Circus

By JAMES OTIS

Illustrations by GEORGE WILSON

COMPANION LIBRARY

GROSSET & DUNLAP
PUBLISHERS • NEW YORK

Contents

TOBY TYLER

Toby's Introduction
to the Circus

"COULDN'T YOU give more'n six peanuts for a cent?"
was a question asked by a very small boy, with big,
staring eyes, of a candy vendor at a circus booth.
And as he spoke, he looked wistfully at the quantity
of nuts piled high up on the basket, and then at the
six, each of which now looked so small as he held
them in his hand.

"Couldn't do it," was the reply of the proprietor of
the booth, as he put the boy's penny carefully away
in the drawer.

The little fellow looked for another moment at his
purchase, and then carefully cracked the largest one.

A shade—and a very deep shade it was—of disappointment passed over his face, and then, looking up
anxiously, he asked, "Don't you swap 'em when
they're bad?"

The man's face looked as if a smile had been a
stranger to it for a long time; but one did pay it a
visit just then, and he tossed the boy two nuts and

asked him a question at the same time. "What is your name?"

The big, brown eyes looked up for an instant, as if to learn whether the question was asked in good faith, and then their owner said, as he carefully picked apart another nut, "Toby Tyler."

"Well, that's a queer name."

"Yes, I s'pose so, myself; but, you see, I don't expect that's the name that belongs to me. But the fellers call me so, an' so does Uncle Dan'l."

"Who is Uncle Daniel?" was the next question. In the absence of other customers the man seemed disposed to get as much amusement out of the boy as possible.

"He hain't my uncle at all; I only call him so because all the boys do, an' I live with him."

"Where's your father and mother?"

"I don't know," said Toby, rather carelessly. "I don't know much about 'em, an' Uncle Dan'l says they don't know much about me. Here's another bad nut; goin' to give me two more?"

The two nuts were given him, and he said, as he put them in his pocket and turned over and over again those which he held in his hand, "I shouldn't wonder if all of these was bad. S'posen you give me two for each one of 'em before I crack 'em, an' they won't be spoiled so you can't sell 'em again."

As this offer of barter was made, the man looked amused, and he asked, as he counted out the number which Toby desired, "If I give you these, I suppose you'll want me to give you two more for each one, and you'll keep that kind of trade going until you get my whole stock?"

"I won't open my head if every one of 'em's bad."

"All right; you can keep what you've got, and I'll give you these besides; but I don't want you to buy any more, for I don't want to do that kind of business."

Toby took the nuts offered, not in the least abashed, and seated himself on a convenient stone to eat them and at the same time to see all that was going on around him. The coming of a circus to the little town of Guilford was an event, and Toby had hardly thought of anything else since the highly colored posters had first been put up. It was yet quite early in the morning, and the tents were just being erected by the men. Toby had followed, with eager eyes, everything that looked as if it belonged to the circus, from the time the first wagon had entered the town until the street parade had been made and everything was being prepared for the afternoon's performance.

The man who had made the losing trade in peanuts seemed disposed to question the boy still further, probably owing to the fact that he had nothing better to do.

"Who is this Uncle Daniel you say you live with? Is he a farmer?"

"No; he's a deacon, an' he raps me over the head with the hymn book whenever I go to sleep in meetin', an' he says I eat four times as much as I earn. I blame him for hittin' so hard when I go to sleep, but I s'pose he's right about my eatin'. You see," and here his tone grew both confidential and mournful, "I am an awful eater, an' I can't seem to help it. Somehow I'm hungry all the time. I don't seem ever to get enough till carrot time comes, an' then I can get all I want without troublin' anybody."

"Didn't you ever have enough to eat?"

"I s'pose I did; but you see Uncle Dan'l he found me one mornin' on his hay, an' he says I was cryin' for something to eat then, an' I've kept it up ever since. I tried to get him to give me money enough to go into the circus with; but he said a cent was all he could spare these hard times, an' I'd better take that an' buy something to eat with it, for the show wasn't very good, anyway. I wish peanuts wasn't but a cent a bushel."

"Then you would make yourself sick eating them."

"Yes, I s'pose I should; Uncle Dan'l says I'd eat till I was sick, if I got the chance; but I'd like to try it once."

He was a very small boy, with a round head covered with short red hair, a face as speckled as any turkey's egg, but thoroughly good-natured looking. As he sat there on the rather sharp point of the rock, swaying his body to and fro as he hugged his knees with his hands and kept his eyes fastened on the tempting display of good things before him, it would have been a very hard-hearted man who would not have given him something. But Mr. Job Lord, the proprietor of the booth, was a hard-hearted man, and he did not make the slightest advance toward offering the little fellow anything.

Toby rocked himself silently for a moment, and then he said hesitatingly, "I don't suppose you'd like to sell me some things, an' let me pay you when I get older, would you?"

Mr. Lord shook his head decidedly at this proposition.

"I didn't s'pose you would," said Toby quickly, "but you didn't seem to be selling anything, an' I thought I'd just see what you'd say about it." And then he appeared suddenly to see something wonderfully interesting behind him, which served as an excuse to turn his reddening face away.

"I suppose your Uncle Daniel makes you work for your living, don't he?" asked Mr. Lord, after he had

[4]

rearranged his stock of candy and had added a couple of slices of lemon peel to what was popularly supposed to be lemonade.

"That's what I think; but he says that all the work I do wouldn't pay for the meal that one chicken would eat, an' I s'pose it's so, for I don't like to work as well as a feller without any father and mother ought to. I don't know why it is, but I guess it's because I take up so much time eatin' that it kinder tires me out. I s'pose you go into the circus whenever you want to, don't you?"

"Oh, yes; I'm there at every performance, for I keep the stand under the big canvas as well as this one out here."

There was a great big sigh from out Toby's little round stomach, as he thought what bliss it must be to own all those good things and to see the circus wherever it went. "It must be nice," he said, as he faced the booth and its hard-visaged proprietor once more.

"How would you like it?" asked Mr. Lord patronizingly, as he looked Toby over in a business way, very much as if he contemplated purchasing him.

"Like it!" echoed Toby, "why, I would grow fat on it."

"I don't know as that that would be any advantage," continued Mr. Lord reflectively, "for it strikes me that you're about as fat now as a boy of your age ought to be. But I've a great mind to give you a chance."

"What!" cried Toby, in amazement, and his eyes opened to their widest extent, as this possible opportunity of leading a delightful life presented itself.

"Yes, I've a great mind to give you the chance. You see," and now it was Mr. Lord's turn to grow confidential, "I've had a boy with me this season, but he cleared out at the last town, and I'm running the business alone now."

Toby's face expressed all the contempt he felt for the boy who would run away from such a glorious life as Mr. Lord's assistant must lead, but he said not a word, waiting in breathless expectation for the offer which he now felt certain would be made him.

"Now I ain't hard on a boy," continued Mr. Lord, still confidentially, "and yet that one seemed to think that he was treated worse and made to work harder than any boy in the world."

"He ought to live with Uncle Dan'l a week," said Toby eagerly.

"Here I was just like a father to him," said Mr. Lord, paying no attention to the interruption, "and I gave him his board and lodging and a dollar a week besides."

"Could he do what he wanted to with the dollar?"

"Of course he could. I never checked him, no matter how extravagant he was, an' yet I've seen him spend his whole week's wages at this very stand in one afternoon. And even after his money had all gone that way, I've paid for peppermint and ginger out of my own pocket just to cure his stomachache."

Toby shook his head mournfully, as if deploring that depravity which could cause a boy to run away from such a tender-hearted employer and from such a desirable position. But even as he shook his head so sadly, he looked wistfully at the peanuts, and Mr. Lord observed the look.

It may have been that Mr. Job Lord was the tender-hearted man he prided himself upon being, or it may have been that he wished to purchase Toby's sympathy; but, at all events, he gave him a large handful of nuts, and Toby never bothered his little round head as to what motive prompted the gift. Now

[6]

he could listen to the story of the boy's treachery and eat at the same time; therefore he was an attentive listener.

"All in the world that boy had to do," continued Mr. Lord, in the same injured tone he had previously used, "was to help me set things to rights when we struck a town in the morning, and then tend to the counter till we left the town at night, and all the rest of the time he had to himself. Yet that boy was ungrateful enough to run away."

Mr. Lord paused, as if expecting some expression of sympathy from his listener; but Toby was so busily engaged with his unexpected feast, and his mouth was so full that it did not seem even possible for him to shake his head.

"Now what should you say if I told you that you looked to me like a boy that was made especially to help run a candy counter at a circus, and if I offered the place to you?"

Toby made one frantic effort to swallow the very large mouthful, and in a choking voice he answered quickly, "I should say I'd go with you, an' be mighty glad of the chance."

"Then it's a bargain, my boy, and you shall leave town with me tonight."

[2]

Toby Runs Away from Home

TOBY COULD scarcely restrain himself at the prospect of this golden future that had so suddenly opened before him. He tried to express his gratitude, but could only do so by evincing his willingness to commence work at once.

"No, no, that won't do," said Mr. Lord cautiously. "If your Uncle Daniel should see you working here, he might mistrust something, and then you couldn't get away."

"I don't believe he'd try to stop me," said Toby confidently, "for he's told me lots of times that it was a sorry day for him when he found me."

"We won't take any chances, my son," was the reply, in a very benevolent tone, as he patted Toby on the head and at the same time handed him a piece of pasteboard. "There's a ticket for the circus, and you come around to see me about ten o'clock tonight. I'll put you on one of the wagons, and by tomorrow morning your Uncle Daniel will have hard work to find you."

If Toby had followed his inclinations, the chances are that he would have fallen on his knees and kissed Mr. Lord's hands in the excess of his gratitude. But not knowing exactly how such a show of thankfulness might be received, he contented himself by repeatedly promising that he would be punctual to the time and place appointed.

He would have loitered in the vicinity of the candy stand in order that he might gain some insight into the business, but Mr. Lord advised that he remain away, lest his Uncle Daniel should see him and suspect where he had gone when he was missed in the morning.

As Toby walked around the circus grounds, whereon was so much to attract his attention, he could not prevent himself from assuming an air of proprietorship. His interest in all that was going on was redoubled, and in his anxiety that everything should be done correctly and in the proper order he actually, and perhaps for the first time in his life, forgot that he was hungry. He was really to travel with a circus, to become a part, as it were, of the whole, and to be able to see its many wonderful and beautiful attractions every day.

Even the very tent ropes had acquired a new interest for him, and the faces of the men at work seemed suddenly to have become those of friends. How hard it was for him to walk around unconcernedly: and how especially hard to prevent his feet from straying toward that tempting display of dainties which he was to sell to those who came to see and enjoy, and who would look at him with wonder and curiosity! It was very hard not to be allowed to tell his playmates of his wonderfully good fortune; but silence meant success, and he locked his secret in his bosom, not even daring to talk with anyone he knew, lest he should betray himself by some incautious word.

He did not go home to dinner that day, and once or twice he felt impelled to walk past the candy stand, giving a mysterious shake of the head at the proprietor as he did so. The afternoon performance passed off as usual to all of the spectators save Toby. He imagined that each one of the performers knew that he was about to join them; even as he passed the cage containing the monkeys, he fancied that one particularly old one knew all about his intention of running away.

Of course it was necessary for him to go home at the close of the afternoon's performance, in order to get one or two valuable articles of his own, such as a boat, a kite, and a pair of skates, and in order that his actions might not seem suspicious. Before he left the grounds, however, he stole slyly around to the candy stand and informed Mr. Job Lord in a very hoarse whisper that he would be on hand at the time appointed.

Mr. Lord patted him on the head, gave him two large sticks of candy, and, what was more kind and surprising, considering the fact that he wore glasses and was cross-eyed, he winked at Toby. A wink from Mr. Lord must have been intended to convey a great deal, because, owing to the defect in his eyes, it required no little exertion, and even then could not be considered as a really first-class wink.

That wink, distorted as it was, gladdened Toby's heart immensely and took away nearly all the sting of the scolding with which Uncle Daniel greeted him when he reached home.

That night, despite the fact that he was going to travel with the circus, despite the fact that his home was not a happy or cheerful one, Toby was not in a pleasant frame of mind. He began to feel for the first time that he was doing wrong. And as he gazed at Uncle Daniel's stern, forbidding-looking face, it seemed to have changed somewhat from its severity, and caused a great lump of something to come up in his throat as he thought that perhaps he should never see it again. Just then one or two kind words would have prevented him from running away, bright as the prospect of circus life appeared.

It was almost impossible for him to eat anything, and this very surprising state of affairs attracted the attention of Uncle Daniel.

"Bless my heart! What ails the boy?" asked the old man, as he peered over his glasses at Toby's well-filled plate, which was usually emptied so quickly. "Are ye sick, Toby, or what is the matter with ye?"

"No, I hain't sick," said Toby with a sigh, "but I've been to the circus, an' I got a good deal to eat."

"Oho! You spent that cent I give ye, eh, an' got so much that it made ye sick?"

Toby thought of the six peanuts which he had bought with the penny Uncle Daniel had given him; and, amid all his homesickness, he could not help wondering if Uncle Daniel ever made himself sick with only six peanuts when he was a boy.

As no one paid any further attention to Toby, he pushed back his plate, arose from the table, and went with a heavy heart to attend to his regular evening chores. The cow, the hens, and even the pigs came in for a share of his unusually kind attention; and as he fed them all, the big tears rolled down his cheeks as he thought that perhaps never again would he see any of them. These dumb animals had all been Toby's confidants; he had poured out his griefs in their ears and fancied, when the world or Uncle Daniel had used him unusually hard, that they sympathized with him. Now he was leaving them forever, and as he locked the stable door, he could hear the sounds of music coming from the direction of the circus grounds, and he was angry at it, because it represented that which was taking him away from his home, even though it was not as pleasant as it might have been.

Still, he had no thought of breaking the engagement which he had made. He went to his room, made a bundle of his worldly possessions, and crept out of the back door, down the road to the circus.

Mr. Lord saw him as soon as he arrived on the grounds, and as he passed another ticket to Toby, he took his bundle from him, saying, as he did so, "I'll pack up your bundle with my things, and then you'll be sure not to lose it. Don't you want some candy?"

Toby shook his head; he had just discovered that there was possibly some connection between his heart and his stomach, for his grief at leaving home had taken from him all desire for good things. It is also more than possible that Mr. Lord had had experience enough with boys to know that they might be homesick on the eve of starting to travel with a circus; and in order to make sure that Toby would keep to his engagement, he was unusually kind.

That evening was the longest that Toby ever knew. He wandered from one cage of animals to another, then to see the performance in the ring, and back again to the animals, in the vain hope of passing the time pleasantly. But it was of no use; that lump in his throat would remain there, and the thoughts of what he was about to do would trouble him severely. The performance failed to interest him, and the animals did not attract until he had visited the monkey cage for the third or fourth time. Then he fancied that the same venerable monkey who had looked so knowing

*He crept out of the back door, down the road
to the circus*

in the afternoon was gazing at him with a sadness which could only have come from a thorough knowledge of all the grief and doubt that was in his heart.

There was no one around the cages, and Toby got just as near to the iron bars as possible. No sooner had he flattened his little pug nose against the iron than the aged monkey came down from the ring in which he had been swinging, and, seating himself directly in front of Toby's face, looked at him most compassionately.

It would not have surprised the boy just then if the animal had spoken; but as he did not, Toby did the next best thing and spoke to him.

"I s'pose you remember that you saw me this afternoon, an' somebody told you that I was goin' to join the circus, didn't they?"

The monkey made no reply, though Toby fancied that he winked an affirmative answer; and he looked so sympathetic that he continued, confidentially:

"Well, I'm the same feller, an' I don't mind telling you that I'm awfully sorry I promised that candy man I'd go with him. Do you know that I came near crying at the supper table tonight; an' Uncle Dan'l looked real good an' nice, though I never thought so before. I wish I wasn't goin', after all, 'cause it don't seem a bit like a good time now. But I s'pose I must, 'cause I promised to, an' 'cause the candy man has got all my things."

The big tears had begun to roll down Toby's cheeks, and as he ceased speaking, the monkey reached out one little paw, which Toby took as earnestly as if it had been done purposely to console him.

"You're real good, you are," continued Toby, "an' I hope I shall see you real often, for it seems to me now, when there hain't any folks around, as if you

[14]

was the only friend I've got in this great big world. It's awful when a feller feels the way I do, an' when he don't seem to want anything to eat. Now if you'll stick to me, I'll stick to you, an' then it won't be half so bad when we feel this way."

During this speech Toby had still clung to the little brown paw, which the monkey now withdrew and continued to gaze into the boy's face.

"The fellers all say I don't amount to anything," sobbed Toby, "an' Uncle Dan'l says I don't, an' I s'pose they know; but I tell you I feel just as bad, now that I'm goin' away from them all, as if I was as good as any of them."

At this moment Toby saw Mr. Lord enter the tent, and he knew that the summons to start was about to be given.

"Good-by," he said to the monkey, as he vainly tried to take him by the hand again, "remember what I've told you, an' don't forget that Toby Tyler is feelin' worse tonight than if he was twice as big an' twice as good."

Mr. Lord had come to summon him away, and he now told Toby that he would show him with which man he was to ride that night.

Toby looked another good-by at the venerable monkey, who was watching him closely, and then followed his employer out of the tent, among the ropes and poles and general confusion attendant upon the removal of a circus from one place to another.

[3]

The Night Ride

THE WAGON on which Mr. Lord was to send his new-found employee was, by the most singular chance, the one containing the monkeys, and Toby accepted this as a good omen. He would be near his venerable friend all night, and there was some consolation in that. The driver instructed the boy to watch his movements, and when he saw him leading his horses around, "To look lively, and be on hand, for he never waited for anyone."

Toby not only promised to do as ordered, but he followed the driver around so closely that, had he desired, he could not have rid himself of his little companion.

The scene which presented itself to Toby's view was strange and weird in the extreme. Shortly after he had attached himself to the man with whom he was to ride, the performance was over, and the work of putting the show and its belongings into such a shape as could be conveyed from one town to another was soon in active operation. Toby forgot his grief, forgot that he was running away from the only home he had ever known, in fact, forgot everything concerning himself, so interested was he in that which was going on about him.

As soon as the audience had got out of the tent— and almost before—the work of taking down the canvas was begun.

Torches were stuck in the earth at regular intervals, the lights that had shone so brilliantly in and around the ring had been extinguished, the canvas sides had been taken off, and the boards that had formed the seats were being packed into one of the carts with a rattling sound that seemed as if a regular fusillade of musketry was being indulged in. Men were shouting, horses were being driven hither and thither, harnessed to the wagons, or drawing the huge carts away as soon as they were loaded. Everything seemed in the greatest state of confusion, while really the work was being done in the most systematic manner possible.

Toby had not long to wait before the driver informed him that the time for starting had arrived and assisted him to climb up to the narrow seat whereon he was to ride that night.

The scene was so exciting, and his efforts to stick to the narrow seat so great, that he really had no time to attend to the homesick feeling that had crept over him during the first part of the evening.

The long procession of carts and wagons drove slowly out of the town, and when the last familiar house had been passed, the driver spoke to Toby for the first time since they started.

"Pretty hard work to keep on—eh, sonny?"

"Yes," replied the boy, as the wagon jolted over a rock, bouncing him high in air, and he by strenuous efforts, barely succeeded in alighting on the seat again, "it is pretty hard work; an' my name's Toby Tyler."

Toby heard a queer sound that seemed to come from the man's throat, and for a few moments he feared that his companion was choking. But he soon understood that this was simply an attempt to laugh, and he at once decided that it was a very poor style of laughing.

"So you object to being called sonny, do you?"

"Well, I'd rather be called Toby, for, you see, that's my name."

"All right, my boy, we'll call you Toby. I suppose you thought it was a mighty fine thing to run away an' jine a circus, didn't you?"

Toby started in affright, looked around cautiously, and then tried to peer down through the small, square aperture, guarded by iron rods, that opened into the cage just back of the seat they were sitting on. Then he turned slowly around to the driver and asked in a voice sunk to a whisper, "How did you know that I was runnin' away? Did he tell you?" and Toby motioned with his thumb as if he were pointing out someone behind him.

It was the driver's turn now to look around in search of the "he" referred to by Toby.

"Who do you mean?" asked the man impatiently.

"Why, the old feller; the one in the cart there. I think he knew I was runnin' away, though he didn't say anything about it; but he looked just as if he did."

The driver looked at Toby in perfect amazement for a moment, and then, as if suddenly understanding the boy, relapsed into one of those convulsive efforts that caused the blood to rush up into his face and gave him every appearance of having a fit.

"You must mean one of the monkeys," said the driver, after he had recovered his breath, which had been almost shaken out of his body by the silent laughter. "So you thought a monkey had told me what any fool could have seen if he had watched you for five minutes."

"Well," said Toby slowly, as if he feared he might provoke one of those terrible laughing spells again, "I saw him tonight, an' he looked as if he knew what I was doin'; so I up an' told him, an' I didn't know but he'd told you, though he didn't look to me like a feller that would be mean."

There was another internal shaking on the part of the driver, which Toby did not fear so much, since he was getting accustomed to it, and then the man said, "Well, you are the queerest little cove I ever saw."

"I s'pose I am," was the reply, accompanied by a long-drawn sigh. "I don't seem to amount to so much as the other fellers do, an' I guess it's because I'm always hungry. You see, I eat awful, Uncle Dan'l says."

The only reply which the driver made to this plaintive confession was to put his hand down into the deepest recesses of one of his deep pockets and to draw therefrom a huge doughnut, which he handed to his companion.

Toby was so much at his ease by this time that the appetite which had failed him at supper had now returned in full force, and he devoured the doughnut in a most ravenous manner.

"You're too small to eat so fast," said the man in a warning tone, as the last morsel of the greasy sweetness disappeared, and he fished up another for the boy. "Some time you'll get hold of one of the India-rubber doughnuts that they feed to circus people, an' choke yourself to death."

Toby shook his head and devoured this second

cake as quickly as he had the first, craning his neck and uttering a funny little squeak as the last bit went down, just as a chicken does when he gets too large a mouthful of dough.

"I'll never choke," he said confidently, "I'm used to it. And Uncle Dan'l says I could eat a pair of boots an' never wink at 'em; but I don't just believe that."

As the driver made no reply to this remark, Toby curled himself up on one corner of the seat and watched with no little interest all that was passing on around him. Each of the wagons had a lantern fastened to the hind axle, and these lights could be seen far ahead on the road, as if a party of fireflies had started in single file on an excursion. The trees by the side of the road stood out weird and ghostly looking in the darkness, and the rumble of the carts ahead and behind formed a musical accompaniment to the picture that sounded strangely doleful.

Mile after mile was passed over in perfect silence, save now and then when the driver would whistle a few bars of some very dismal tune that would fairly make Toby shiver with its mournfulness. Eighteen miles was the distance from Guilford to the town where the next performance of the circus was to be given, and as Toby thought of the ride before them, it seemed as if the time would be almost interminable. He curled himself up on one corner of the seat and tried very hard to go to sleep; but just as his eyes began to grow heavy, the wagon would jolt over some rock or sink deep in some rut, till Toby, the breath very nearly shaken out of his body and his neck almost dislocated, would sit bolt upright, clinging to the seat with both hands, as if he expected each moment to be pitched out into the mud.

The driver watched him closely and each time that he saw him shaken up and awakened so thoroughly, he would indulge in one of his silent laughing spells, until Toby would wonder whether he would ever recover from it. Several times had Toby been awakened, and each time he had seen the amusement his sufferings caused, until he finally resolved to put an end to the sport by keeping awake.

"What is your name?" he asked of the driver, thinking a conversation would be the best way to rouse himself into wakefulness.

"Waal," said the driver, as he gathered the reins carefully in one hand and seemed to be debating in his mind how he should answer the question, "I don't know as I know myself, it's been so long since I've heard it."

Toby was wide enough awake now, as this rather singular problem was forced upon his mind. He revolved the matter silently for some moments, and at last he asked, "What do folks call you when they want to speak to you?"

"They always call me Old Ben, an' I've got so used to the name that I don't need any other."

Toby wanted very much to ask more questions, but he wisely concluded that it would not be agreeable to his companion.

"I'll ask the old man about it," said Toby to himself, referring to the aged monkey, whom he seemed to feel acquainted with. "He most likely knows, if he'll say anything." After this the conversation ceased, until Toby again ventured to suggest, "It's a pretty long drive, hain't it?"

"You want to wait till you've been in this business a year or two," said Ben sagely, "an' then you won't think much of it. Why, I've known the show towns to be thirty miles apart, an' them was the times when we had lively work of it. Riding all night and working all day kind of wears on a fellow."

"Yes, I s'pose so," said Toby, with a sigh, as he wondered whether he had got to work as hard as that, "but I s'pose you get all you want to eat, don't you?"

"Now you've struck it!" said Ben, with the air of one about to impart a world of wisdom, as he crossed one leg over the other, that his position might be as comfortable as possible while he was initiating his young companion into the mysteries of the life. "I've had all the boys ride with me since I've been with this show, an' I've tried to start them right; but they didn't seem to profit by it, an' always got sick of the show an' run away, just because they didn't look out for themselves as they ought to. Now listen to me, Toby, an' remember what I say. You see, they put us all in a hotel together, an' some of these places where we go don't have any too much stuff on the table. Whenever we strike a new town, you find out at the hotel what time they have the grub ready, an' you be on hand, so's to get in with the first. Eat all you can, an' fill your pockets."

"If that's all a feller has to do to travel with a circus," said Toby, "I'm just the one, 'cause I always used to do just that when I hadn't any idea of bein' a circus man."

"Then you'll get along all right," said Ben, as he checked the speed of his horses and, looking carefully ahead, said, as he guided his team to one side of the road, "This is as far as we're going tonight."

Toby learned that they were within a couple of miles of the town and that the entire procession would remain by the roadside until time to make the grand entrée into the village, when every wagon, horse, and man would be decked out in the most gorgeous array, as they had been when they entered Guilford.

Under Ben's direction he wrapped himself in an old horse blanket and lay down on the top of the wagon. And he was so tired from the excitement of the day and night, that he had hardly stretched out at full length before he was fast asleep.

[4]

The First Day
with the Circus

WHEN TOBY awakened and looked around, he could
hardly realize where he was or how he came there.
As far ahead and behind on the road as he could see,
the carts were drawn up on one side; men were
hurrying to and fro, orders were being shouted, and
everything showed that the entry into the town was
about to be made. Directly opposite the wagon on
which he had been sleeping were the four elephants
and two camels, and close behind, contentedly
munching their breakfasts, were a number of tiny
ponies. Troops of horses were being groomed and
attended to; the road was littered with saddles, flags,
and general decorations, until it seemed to Toby that
there must have been a smash-up, and that he now
beheld ruins rather than systematic disorder.

How different everything looked now, compared
to the time when the cavalcade marched into Guilford, dazzling everyone with the gorgeous display!
Then the horses pranced gaily under their gaudy
decorations, the wagons were bright with glass, gilt,

and flags, the lumbering elephants and awkward camels were covered with fancifully embroidered velvets, and even the drivers of the wagons were resplendent in their uniforms of scarlet and gold. Now, in the gray light of the early morning, everything was changed. The horses were tired and muddy and wore old and dirty harness. The gilded chariots were covered with mud-bespattered canvas, which caused them to look like the most ordinary of market wagons. The elephants and camels looked dingy, dirty, almost repulsive. And the drivers were only a sleepy-looking set of men, who, in their shirt-sleeves, were getting ready for the change which would dazzle the eyes of the inhabitants of the town.

Toby descended from his lofty bed, rubbed his eyes to awaken himself thoroughly, and under the guidance of Ben went to a little brook nearby and washed his face. He had been with the circus not quite ten hours, but now he could not realize that it had ever seemed bright and beautiful. He missed his comfortable bed, the quiet and cleanliness, and the well-spread table. Although he had felt the lack of a parent's care, Uncle Daniel's home seemed the very abode of love and friendly feeling compared to this condition, where no one appeared to care even enough for him to scold at him. He was thoroughly homesick and heartily wished that he was back in his old native town.

While he was washing his face in the brook, he saw some of the boys who had come out from the town to catch the first glimpse of the circus, and he saw at once that he was the object of their admiring gaze. He heard one of the boys say when they first discovered him:

"There's one of them, an' he's only a little feller; so I'm going to talk to him."

The evident admiration which the boys had for Toby pleased him, and this pleasure was the only drop of comfort he had had since he started. He hoped that they would come and talk with him; and, that they might have the opportunity, he was purposely slow in making his toilet.

The boys approached him shyly, as if they had their doubts whether he was made of the same material as themselves, and when they got quite near to him and satisfied themselves that he was only washing his face in much the same way that any well-regulated boy would do, the one who had called attention to him said, half timidly, "Hello!"

"Hello!" responded Toby, in a tone that was meant to invite confidence.

"Do you belong to the circus?"

"Yes," said Toby a little doubtfully.

Then the boys stared at him again as if he were one of the strange-looking animals, and the one who had been the spokesman drew a long breath of envy as he said longingly, "My! What a nice time you must have!"

Toby remembered that only yesterday he himself had thought that boys must have a nice time with a circus, and he now felt what a mistake that thought was; but he concluded that he would not undeceive his new acquaintance.

"And do they give you frogs to eat, so's to make you limber?"

This was the first time that Toby had thought of breakfast, and the very mention of eating made him hungry. He was just at that moment so very hungry that he did not think he was replying to the question when he said quickly, "Eat frogs! I could eat anything if I only had the chance."

The boys took this as an answer to their question,

and felt perfectly convinced that the agility of circus riders and tumblers depended upon the quantity of frogs eaten, and they looked upon Toby with no little degree of awe.

Toby might have undeceived them as to the kind of food he ate, but just at that moment the harsh voice of Mr. Job Lord was heard calling him, and he hurried away to commence his first day's work.

Toby's employer was not the same pleasant, kindly-spoken man that he had been during the time they were in Guilford and before the boy was absolutely under his control. He looked cross, he acted cross, and it did not take the boy very long to find out that he was very cross.

He scolded Toby roundly and launched more oaths at his defenseless head than Toby had ever heard in his life. He was angry that the boy had not been on hand to help him and also that he had been obliged to hunt for him.

Toby tried to explain that he had no idea of what he was expected to do, and that he had been on the wagon to which he had been sent, only leaving it to wash his face; but the angry man grew still more furious.

"Went to wash your face, did yer? Want to set yourself up for a dandy, I suppose, and think that you must souse that speckled face of yours into every brook you come to? I'll soon break you of that; and the sooner you understand that I can't afford to have you wasting your time in washing, the better it will be for you."

Toby now grew angry, and not realizing how wholly he was in the man's power, he retorted, "If you think I'm going round with a dirty face, even if it is speckled, for a dollar a week, you're mistaken, that's all. How many folks would eat your candy if they knew you handled it over before you washed your hands?"

"Oho! I've picked up a preacher, have I? Now I want you to understand, my bantam, that I do all the preaching as well as the practicing myself, and this is about as quick a way as I know of to make you understand it."

As the man spoke, he grasped the boy by the coat collar with one hand and with the other plied a thin rubber cane with no gentle force to every portion of Toby's body that he could reach.

Every blow caused the poor boy the most intense pain, but he determined that his tormentor should not have the satisfaction of forcing an outcry from him, and he closed his lips so tightly that not a single sound could escape from them.

This very silence enraged the man so much that he redoubled the force and rapidity of his blows, and it is impossible to say what might have been the consequences had not Ben come that way just then and changed the aspect of affairs.

"Up to your old tricks of whipping the boys, are you, Job?" he said, as he wrested the cane from the man's hand and held him off at arm's length, to prevent him from doing Toby more mischief.

Mr. Lord struggled to release himself and insisted that, since the boy was in his employ, he should do with him just as he saw fit.

"Now look here, Mr. Lord," said Ben, as gravely as if he was delivering some profound piece of wisdom, "I've never interfered with you before, but now I'm going to stop your game of thrashing your boy every morning before breakfast. You just tell this youngster what you want him to do, and if he don't do it, you can discharge him. If I hear of your flogging him, I shall attend to your case at once. You hear me?"

[28]

"Up to your old tricks of whipping the boys,
are you, Job?"

Ben shook the now terrified candy vendor much as if he had been a child, and then released him, saying to Toby as he did so, "Now, my boy, you attend to your business as you ought to, and I'll settle his account if he tries the flogging game again."

"You see, I don't know what there is for me to do," sobbed Toby, for the kindly interference of Ben had made him show more feeling than Mr. Lord's blows had done.

"Tell him what he must do," said Ben sternly.

"I want him to go to work and wash the tumblers and fix up the things in that green box, so we can commence to sell as soon as we get into town," snarled Mr. Lord, as he motioned toward a large green chest that had been taken out of one of the carts, and which Toby saw was filled with dirty glasses, spoons, knives, and other utensils such as were necessary to carry on the business.

Toby got a pail of water from the brook, hunted around and found towels and soap, and devoted himself to his work with such industry that Mr. Lord could not repress a grunt of satisfaction as he passed him, however angry he felt because he could not administer the whipping which would have smoothed his ruffled temper.

By the time the procession was ready to start for the town, Toby had as much of his work done as he could find that it was necessary to do, and his master, in his surly way, half acknowledged that this last boy of his was better than any he had had before.

Although Toby had done his work so well, he was far from feeling happy. He was both angry and sad as he thought of the cruel blows that had been inflicted, and he had plenty of leisure to repent of the rash step he had taken, although he could not see very clearly how he was to get away from it. He thought that he could not go back to Guilford, for Uncle Daniel would not allow him to come to his house again, and the hot, scalding tears ran down his cheeks as he realized that he was homeless and friendless in this great big world.

It was while he was in this frame of mind that the procession, all gaudy with flags, streamers, and banners, entered the town. Under different circumstances this would have been a most delightful day for him, for the entrance of a circus into Guilford had always been a source of one day's solid enjoyment; but now he was the most disconsolate and unhappy boy in all that crowd.

He did not ride throughout the entire route of the procession, for Mr. Lord was anxious to begin business, and the moment the tenting ground was reached, the wagon containing Mr. Lord's goods was driven into the enclosure, and Toby's day's work began.

He was obliged to bring water, to cut up the lemons, fetch and carry fruit from the booth in the big tent to the booth on the outside, until he was ready to drop with fatigue, and having had no time for breakfast, was nearly famished.

It was quite noon before he was permitted to go to the hotel for something to eat, and then Ben's advice to be one of the first to get to the tables was not needed.

In the eating line that day he astonished the servants, the members of the company, and even himself, and by the time he arose from the table, with both pockets and his stomach full to bursting, the tables had been set and cleared away twice while he was making one meal.

"Well, I guess you didn't hurry yourself much,"

said Mr. Lord, when Toby returned to the circus ground.

"Oh, yes, I did," was Toby's innocent reply, "I ate just as fast as I could," and a satisfied smile stole over the boy's face as he thought of the amount of solid food which he had consumed.

The answer was not one which was calculated to make Mr. Lord feel any more agreeably disposed toward his new clerk, and he showed his ill-temper very plainly as he said, "It must take a good deal to satisfy you."

"I s'pose it does," calmly replied Toby. "Sam Merrill used to say that I took after Aunt Olive and Uncle Dan'l. One ate a good while, an' the other ate awful fast."

Toby could not understand what it was that Mr. Lord said in reply, but he could understand that his employer was angry at somebody or something, and he tried unusually hard to please him. He talked to the boys who had gathered around, to induce them to buy, washed the glasses as fast as they were used, tried to keep off the flies, and in every way he could think of endeavored to please his master.

[5]

The Counterfeit
Ten-Cent Piece

WHEN THE doors of the big tent were opened and the people began to crowd in, just as Toby had seen them do at Guilford, Mr. Lord announced to his young clerk that it was time for him to go into the tent to work. Then it was that Toby learned for the first time that he had two masters instead of one, and this knowledge caused him no little uneasiness. If the other one was anything like Mr. Lord, his lot would be just twice as bad, and he began to wonder whether he could even stand it one day longer.

As the boy passed through the tent on his way to the candy stand, where he was really to enter upon the duties for which he had run away from home, he wanted to stop for a moment and speak with the old monkey who he thought had taken such an interest in him. But when he reached the cage in which his friend was confined, there was such a crowd around it that it was impossible for him to get near enough to speak without being overheard.

This was such a disappointment to the little fellow

that the big tears came into his eyes, and in another instant would have gone rolling down his cheeks if his aged friend had not chanced to look toward him. Toby fancied that the monkey looked at him in the most friendly way, and then he was certain that he winked one eye. Toby felt that there was no mistake about that wink, and it seemed as if it was intended to convey comfort to him in his troubles. He winked back at the monkey in the most emphatic and grave manner possible and then went on his way, feeling wonderfully comforted.

The work inside the tent was far different and much harder than it was outside. He was obliged to carry around among the audience trays of candy, nuts, and lemonade for sale, and he was also expected to cry aloud the description of that which he offered. The partner of Mr. Lord, who had charge of the stand inside the tent, showed himself to be neither better nor worse than Mr. Lord himself. When Toby first presented himself for work, he handed him a tray filled with glasses of lemonade and told him to go among the audience, crying, "Here's your nice cold lemonade, only five cents a glass!"

Toby started to do as he was bidden; but when he tried to repeat the words in anything like a loud tone of voice, they stuck in his throat, and he found it next to impossible to utter a sound above a whisper. It seemed to him that everyone in the audience was looking only at him, and the very sound of his own voice made him afraid.

He went entirely around the tent once without making a sale, and when he returned to the stand, he was at once convinced that one of his masters was quite as bad as the other. This one—and he knew that his name was Jacobs, for he heard someone call him so—very kindly told him that he would break every bone in his body if he didn't sell something, and Toby confidently believed that he would carry out his threat.

It was with a heavy heart that he started around again in obedience to Mr. Jacob's angry command; but this time he did manage to cry out, in a very thin and very squeaky voice, the words which he had been told to repeat.

This time, perhaps owing to his pitiful and imploring look, certainly not because of the noise he made, he met with very good luck, and sold every glass of the mixture which Messrs. Lord and Jacobs called lemonade and went back to the stand for more.

He certainly thought he had earned a word of praise and fully expected it as he put the empty glasses and money on the stand in front of Mr. Jacobs. But, instead of the kind words, he was greeted with a volley of curses; and the reason for it was that he had taken in payment for two of the glasses a lead ten-cent piece. Mr. Jacobs, after scolding poor little Toby to his heart's content, vowed that the amount should be kept from his first week's wages, and then handed back the coin, with orders to give it to the first man who gave him money to change, under the penalty of a severe flogging if he failed to do so.

Poor Toby tried to explain matters by saying, "You see, I don't know anything about money; I never had more'n a cent at a time, an' you mustn't expect me to get posted all at once."

"I'll post you with a stick if you do it again; an' it won't be well for you if you bring that ten-cent piece back here!"

Now Toby was very well aware that to pass the coin, knowing it to be bad, would be a crime, and he resolved to take the consequences of which Mr. Jacobs had intimated, if he could not find the one who had given him the counterfeit and persuade him to give him good money in its stead. He remembered very plainly where he had sold each glass of lemonade, and he retraced his steps, glancing at each face carefully as he passed. At last he was confident that he saw the man who had gotten him into such trouble, and he climbed up the board seats, saying, as he stood in front of him and held out the coin, "Mister, this money that you gave me is bad. Won't you give me another one for it?"

The man was a rough-looking party who had taken his girl to the circus, and who did not seem at all disposed to pay any heed to Toby's request. Therefore he repeated it, and this time more loudly.

"Get out of the way!" said the man angrily. "How can you expect me to see the show if you stand right in front of me?"

"You'll like it better," said Toby earnestly, "if you give me another ten-cent piece."

"Get out, an' don't bother me!" was the angry rejoinder, and the little fellow began to think that perhaps he would be obliged to "get out" without getting his money.

It was becoming a desperate case, for the man was growing angry very fast, and if Toby did not succeed in getting good money for the bad, he would have to take the consequences of which Mr. Jacobs had spoken.

"Please, mister," he said imploringly, for his heart began to grow very heavy, and he was fearing that he should not succeed, "won't you please give me the money back? You know you gave it to me, an' I'll have to pay it if you don't."

The boy's lip was quivering, and those around

began to be interested in the affair, while several in the immediate vicinity gave vent to their indignation that a man should try to cheat a boy out of ten cents by giving him counterfeit money.

The man whom Toby was speaking to was about to dismiss him with an angry reply, when he saw that those about him were not only interested in the matter but were evidently taking sides with the boy against him. And knowing well that he had given the counterfeit money, he took another coin from his pocket and, handing it to Toby, said, "I didn't give you the lead piece; but you're making such a fuss about it that here's ten cents to make you keep quiet."

"I'm sure you did give me the money," said Toby, as he took the extended coin, "an' I'm much obliged to you for takin' it back. I didn't want to tell you before, 'cause you'd thought I was beggin'; but if you hadn't given me this, I 'xpect I'd have got an awful whippin', for Mr. Jacobs said he'd fix me if I didn't get the money for it."

The man looked sheepish enough as he put the bad money in his pocket, and Toby's innocently told story caused such a feeling in his behalf among those who sat near that he not only disposed of his entire stock then and there, but received from one gentleman twenty-five cents for himself. He was both proud and happy as he returned to Mr. Jacobs with empty glasses, and with the money to refund the amount of loss which would have been caused by the counterfeit.

But the worthy partner of Mr. Lord's candy business had no words of encouragement for the boy who was trying so hard to please.

"Let that make you keep your eyes open," he growled out sulkily, "an' if you get caught in that trap again, you won't be let off so easy."

Poor little Toby! His heart seemed ready to break, but his few hours' previous experience had taught him that there was but one thing to do and that was to work just as hard as possible, trusting to some good fortune to enable him to get out of the very disagreeable position in which he had voluntarily placed himself.

He took the basket of candy that Mr. Jacobs handed him and trudged around the circle of seats, selling far more because of the pitifulness of his face than because of the excellence of his goods; and even this worked to his disadvantage. Mr. Jacobs was keen enough to see why his little clerk sold so many goods, and each time that he returned to the stand he said something to him in an angry tone, which had the effect of deepening the shadow on the boy's face and at the same time increasing trade.

By the time the performance was over, Toby had in his pocket a dollar and twenty-five cents which had been given him for himself by some of the kind-hearted in the audience, and he kept his hand almost constantly upon it, for the money seemed to him like some kind friend who would help him out of his present difficulties.

After the audience had dispersed, Mr. Jacobs set Toby at work washing the glasses and clearing up generally, and then the boy started toward the other portion of the store—that watched over by Mr. Lord. Not a person save the watchmen was in the tent, and as Toby went toward the door, he saw his friend, the monkey, sitting in one corner of the cage and apparently watching his every movement.

It was as if he had suddenly seen one of the boys from home, and Toby, uttering an exclamation of delight, ran up to the cage and put his hand through the wires.

[38]

The monkey, in the gravest possible manner, took one of the fingers in his paw, and Toby shook hands with him very earnestly.

"I was sorry that I couldn't speak to you when I went in this noon," said Toby, as if making an apology, "but, you see, there were so many around here to see you that I couldn't get the chance. Did you see me wink at you?"

The monkey made no reply, but he twisted his face into such a funny little grimace that Toby was quite as well satisfied as if he had spoken.

"I wonder if you hain't some relation to Steve Stubbs?" Toby continued, earnestly, "for you look just like him, only he didn't have quite so many whiskers. What I want to say was, that I'm awful sorry I run away. I used to think that Uncle Dan'l was bad enough, but he was just a perfect good Samarathon to what Mr. Lord an' Mr. Jacobs are. An' when Mr. Lord looks at me with that crooked eye of his, I feel it 'way down in my boots. Do you know"— and here Toby put his mouth nearer to the monkey's head and whispered—"I'd run away from this circus if I could get the chance; wouldn't you?"

Just at this point, as if in answer to the question, the monkey stood up on his hind feet and reached out his paw to the boy, who seemed to think this was his way of being more emphatic in saying, "Yes."

Toby took the paw in his hand, shook it again earnestly, and said as he released it, "I was pretty sure you felt just about the same way I did, Mr. Stubbs, when I passed you this noon. Look here"—and Toby took the money from his pocket which had been given him—"I got all that this afternoon, an' I'll try an' stick it out somehow till I get as much as ten dollars, an' then we'll run away some night, an' go 'way off as far as—as—as out West, an' we'll stay there too."

The monkey, probably tired with remaining in one position so long, started toward the top of the cage, chattering and screaming, joining the other monkeys, who had gathered in a little group in one of the swings.

"Now see here, Mr. Stubbs," said Toby, in alarm, "you mustn't go to telling everybody about it, or Mr. Lord will know, an' then we'll be dished, sure."

The monkey sat quietly in the swing, as if he felt reproved by what the boy had said; and Toby, considerably relieved by his silence, said, as he started toward the door, "That's right—mum's the word; you keep quiet, an' so will I, an' pretty soon we'll get away from the whole crowd."

All the monkeys chattered, and Toby, believing that everything which he had said had been understood by the animals, went out of the door to meet his other taskmaster.

[6]

A Tenderhearted Skeleton

"Now, THEN, lazybones," was Mr. Lord's warning cry as Toby came out of the tent, "if you've fooled away enough of your time, you can come here an' tend shop for me while I go to supper. You crammed yourself this noon, an' it'll teach you a good lesson to make you go without anything to eat tonight. It'll make you move round more lively in future."

Instead of becoming accustomed to such treatment as he was receiving from his employers, Toby's heart grew more tender with each brutal word, and this last punishment—that of losing his supper—caused the poor boy more sorrow than blows would. Mr. Lord started for the hotel as he concluded his cruel speech, and poor little Toby, going behind the counter, leaned his head upon the rough boards and cried as if his heart would break.

All the fancied brightness and pleasure of a circus life had vanished, and in its place was the bitterness of remorse that he had repaid Uncle Daniel's kindness by the ingratitude of running away. Toby thought that if he could only nestle his little red head on the pillows of his little bed in that rough room at Uncle Daniel's, he would be the happiest and best boy in the future, in all the great, wide world.

While he was still sobbing away at a most furious rate, he heard a voice close at his elbow and, looking up, saw the thinnest man he had ever seen in all his life. The man had flesh-colored tights on, and a spangled red velvet garment that was neither pants, because there were no legs to it, nor a coat, because it did not come above his waist, made up the remainder of his costume. Because he was so wonderfully thin, because of the costume which he wore, and because of a highly colored painting which was hanging in front of one of the small tents, Toby knew that the Living Skeleton was before him, and his big, brown eyes opened all the wider as he gazed at him.

"What is the matter, little fellow?" asked the man in a kindly tone. "What makes you cry so? Has Job been up to his old tricks again?"

"I don't know what his old tricks are," and Toby sobbed, the tears coming again because of the sympathy which this man's voice expressed for him, "but I know that he's a mean, ugly thing—that's what I know. An' if I could only get back to Uncle Dan'l, there hain't elephants enough in all the circuses in the world to pull me away again."

"Oh, you run away from home, did you?"

"Yes, I did," sobbed Toby, "an' there hain't any boy in any Sunday-school book that ever I read that was half so sorry he'd been bad as I am. It's awful, an' now I can't have any supper, 'cause I stopped to talk with Mr. Stubbs."

"Is Mr. Stubbs one of your friends?" asked the skeleton as he seated himself in Mr. Lord's own private chair.

"Yes, he is, an' he's the only one in this whole circus who 'pears to be sorry for me. You'd better not let Mr. Lord see you sittin' in that chair or he'll raise a row."

"Job won't raise any row with me," said the skeleton. "But who is this Mr. Stubbs? I don't seem to know anybody by that name."

"I don't think that is his name. I only call him so, 'cause he looks so much like a feller I know who is named Stubbs."

This satisfied the skeleton that this Mr. Stubbs must be someone attached to the show, and he asked:

"Has Job been whipping you?"

"No; Ben, the driver on the wagon where I ride, told him not to do that again; but he hain't going to let me have any supper, 'cause I was so slow about my work—though I wasn't slow. I only talked to Mr. Stubbs when there wasn't anybody round his cage."

"Sam! Sam! Sam-u-el!"

This name, which was shouted twice in a quick, loud voice and the third time in a slow manner, ending almost in a screech, did not come from either Toby or the skeleton, but from an enormously large woman, dressed in a gaudy red-and-black dress, cut very short and with low neck and an apology for sleeves, who had just come out from the tent whereon the picture of the Living Skeleton hung.

"Samuel," she screamed again, "come inside this minute, or you'll catch your death o' cold, an' I shall have you wheezin' around with the phthisic all night. Come in, Sam-u-el."

"That's her," said the skeleton to Toby, as he pointed his thumb in the direction of the fat woman, but paying no attention to the outcry she was making, "that's my wife, Lilly, an' she's the Fat Woman of the show. She's always yellin' after me that way the minute I get out for a little fresh air, an' she's always sayin' just the same thing. Bless you, I never have the phthisic, but she does awful. An' I s'pose 'cause she's so large she can't feel all over her, an' thinks it's me that has it."

"Is—is all that—is that your wife?" stammered Toby, in astonishment, as he looked at the enormously fat woman who stood in the tent door and then at the wonderfully thin man who sat beside him.

"Yes, that's her," said the skeleton. "She weighs pretty nigh four hundred, though of course the show cards says it's over six hundred, an' she earns almost as much money as I do. Of course she can't get so much, for skeletons is much scarcer than fat folks; but we make a pretty good thing travelin' together."

"Sam-u-el!" again came the cry from the fat woman, "are you never coming in?"

"Not yet, my angel," said the skeleton placidly, as he crossed one thin leg over the other and looked calmly at her. "Come here an' see Job's new boy."

"Your imprudence is wearin' me away so that I sha'n't be worth five dollars a week to any circus," she said impatiently, at the same time coming toward the candy stand quite as rapidly as her very great size would admit.

"This is my wife Lilly—Mrs. Treat," said the skeleton, with a proud wave of his hand, as he rose from his seat and gazed admiringly at her. "This is my flower—my queen, Mr.—Mr.—"

"Tyler," said Toby, supplying the name which the skeleton—or Mr. Treat, as Toby now learned his name was—did not know. "Tyler is my name—Toby Tyler."

"Why, what a little chap you are!" said Mrs. Treat,

paying no attention to the awkward little bend of the head which Toby intended for a bow. "How small he is, Samuel!"

"Yes," said the skeleton reflectively, as he looked Toby over from head to foot, as if he were mentally trying to calculate exactly how many inches high he was, "he is small; but he's got all the world before him to grow in, an' if he only eats enough— There, that reminds me. Job isn't going to give him any supper, because he didn't work hard enough."

"He won't, won't he?" exclaimed the large lady savagely. "Oh, he's a precious one, he is. An' some day I shall just give him a good shakin'-up, that's what I'll do. I get all out of patience with that man's ugliness."

"An' she'll do just what she says," said the skeleton to Toby, with an admiring shake of the head. "That woman hain't afraid of anybody, an' I wouldn't be a bit surprised if she did give Job a pretty rough time."

Toby thought, as he looked at her, that she was large enough to give 'most anyone a pretty rough time, but he did not venture to say so. While he was looking first at her and then at her very thin husband, the skeleton told his wife the little that he had learned regarding the boy's history; and when he had concluded, she waddled away toward her tent.

"Great woman that," said the skeleton, as he saw her disappear within the tent.

"Yes," said Toby," she's the greatest I ever saw."

"I mean that she's got a great head. Now you'll see about how much she cares for what Job says."

"If I was as big as her," said Toby, with just a shade of envy in his voice, "I wouldn't be afraid of anybody."

"It hain't so much the size," said the skeleton

sagely, "it hain't so much the size, my boy; for I can scare that woman almost to death when I feel like it."

Toby looked for a moment at Mr. Treat's thin legs and arms and then he said warningly, "I wouldn't feel like it very often if I was you, Mr. Treat, 'cause she might break some of your bones if you didn't happen to scare her enough."

"Don't fear for me, my boy—don't fear for me. You'll see how I manage her if you stay with the circus long enough. Now, I often—"

If Mr. Treat was about to confide a family secret to Toby, it was fated that he should not hear it then, for Mrs. Treat had just come out of her tent, carrying in her hands a large tin plate piled high with a miscellaneous assortment of pie, cake, bread, and meat.

She placed this in front of Toby, and as she did so, she handed him two pictures.

"There, little Toby Tyler," she said, "there's something for you to eat, if Mr. Job Lord and his precious partner Jacobs did say you shouldn't have any supper; an' I've brought you a picture of Samuel an' me. We sell 'em for ten cents apiece, but I'm going to give them to you, because I like the looks of you."

Toby was quite overcome with the presents and seemed at a loss how to thank her for them. He attempted to speak but could not get the words out at first. Then he said, as he put the two photographs in the same pocket with his money, "You're awful good to me, an' when I get to be a man, I'll give you lots of things. I wasn't so very hungry, if I am such a big eater, but I did want something."

"Bless your dear little heart, and you *shall* have something to eat," said the Fat Woman, as she seized Toby, squeezed him close up to her, and kissed his

freckled face as kindly as if it had been as fair and
white as possible. "You shall eat all you want to; an'
if you get the stomachache, as Samuel does sometimes when he's been eatin' too much, I'll give you
some catnip tea out of the same dipper that I give
him his. He's a great eater, Samuel is," she added, in
a burst of confidence, "an' it's a wonder to me what
he does with it all sometimes."

"Is he?" exclaimed Toby quickly. "How funny that
is, for I'm an awful eater. Why, Uncle Dan'l used to
say that I ate twice as much as I ought to, an' it
never made me any bigger. I wonder what's the
reason?"

"I declare I don't know," said the Fat Woman
thoughtfully, "an' I've wondered at it time an' time
again. Some folks is made that way, an' some folks is
made different. Now, I don't eat enough to keep a
chicken alive, an' yet I grow fatter an' fatter every
day. Don't I, Samuel?"

"Indeed you do, my love," said the skeleton, with a
world of pride in his voice, "but you mustn't feel bad
about it, for every pound you gain makes you worth
just so much more to the show."

"Oh, I wasn't worryin', I was only wonderin'. But
we must go, Samuel, for the poor child won't eat a bit
while we are here. After you've eaten what there is
there, bring the plate in to me," she said to Toby, as
she took her lean husband by the arm and walked
him off toward their own tent.

Toby gazed after them a moment, and then he
commenced a vigorous attack upon the eatables
which had been so kindly given him. Of the food
which he had taken from the dinner table he had
eaten some while he was in the tent, and after that he
had entirely forgotten that he had any in his pocket;
therefore, at the time that Mrs. Treat had brought

him such a liberal supply he was really very hungry.

He succeeded in eating nearly all the food which had been brought to him, and the very small quantity which remained he readily found room for in his pockets. Then he washed the plate nicely, and seeing no one in sight, he thought he could leave the booth long enough to return the plate.

He ran with it quickly into the tent occupied by the thin man and fat woman and handed it to her, with a profusion of thanks for her kindness.

"Did you eat it all?" she asked.

"Well," hesitated Toby, "there was three doughnuts an' a piece of pie left over, an' I put them in my pocket. If you don't care, I'll eat them some time tonight."

"You shall eat it whenever you want to, an' any time that you get hungry again, you come right to me."

"Thank you, ma'am. I must go now, for I left the store all alone."

"Run, then; an' if Job Lord abuses you, just let me know it, an' I'll keep him from cuttin' up any monkey shines."

Toby hardly heard the end of her sentence, so great was his haste to get back to the booth. And just as he emerged from the tent on a quick run, he received a blow on the ear which sent him sprawling in the dust, and he heard Mr. Job Lord's angry voice as it said, "So, just the moment my back is turned, you leave the stand to take care of itself, do you, an' run around tryin' to plot some mischief against me, eh?" And the brute kicked the prostrate boy twice with his heavy boot.

"Please don't kick me again!" pleaded Toby. "I wasn't gone but a minute, an' I wasn't doing anything bad."

[48]

"You're lying now, an' you know it, you young cub!" exclaimed the angry man as he advanced to kick the boy again. "I'll let you know who you've got to deal with when you get hold of me!"

"And I'll let you know who you've got to deal with when you get hold of me!" said a woman's voice, and, just as Mr. Lord raised his foot to kick the boy again, the Fat Woman seized him by the collar, jerked him back over one of the tent ropes, and left him quite as prostrate as he had left Toby. "Now, Job Lord," said the angry woman, as she towered above the thoroughly frightened man, "I want you to understand that you can't knock and beat this boy while I'm around. I've seen enough of your capers, an' I'm going to put a stop to them. That boy wasn't in this tent more than two minutes, an' he attends to his work better than anyone you have ever had, so see that you treat him decent. Get up," she said to Toby, who had not dared to rise from the ground, "and if he offers to strike you again, come to me."

Toby scrambled to his feet and ran to the booth in time to attend to one or two customers who had just come up. He could see from out the corner of his eye that Mr. Lord had arisen to his feet also and was engaged in an angry conversation with Mrs. Treat, the result of which he very much feared would be another and a worse whipping for him.

But in this he was mistaken, for Mr. Lord, after the conversation was ended, came toward the booth and began to attend to his business without speaking one word to Toby. When Mr. Jacobs returned from his supper, Mr. Lord took him by the arm and walked him out toward the rear of the tents; and Toby was very positive that he was to be the subject of their conversation, which made him not a little uneasy.

It was not until nearly time for the performance to

begin that Mr. Lord returned and he had nothing to say to Toby, save to tell him to go into the tent and begin his work there. The boy was only too glad to escape so easily, and he went to his work with as much alacrity as if he were about entering upon some pleasure.

When he met Mr. Jacobs, that gentleman spoke to him very sharply about being late and seemed to think it no excuse at all that he had just been relieved from the outside work by Mr. Lord.

[7]

An Accident
and Its Consequences

TOBY'S EXPERIENCE in the evening was very similar to
that of the afternoon, save that he was so fortunate
as not to take any more bad money in payment for
his goods. Mr. Jacobs scolded and swore alternately,
and the boy really surprised him by his way of
selling goods, though he was very careful not to say
anything about it, but made Toby believe that he was
doing only about half as much work as he ought to
do. Toby's private hoard of money was increased that
evening, by presents, ninety cents, and he began to
look upon himself as almost a rich man.

When the performance was nearly over, Mr.
Jacobs called to him to help in packing up; and by
the time the last spectator had left the tent, the
worldly possessions of Messrs. Lord and Jacobs were
ready for removal, and Toby allowed to do as he had
a mind to, as long as he was careful to be on hand
when Old Ben was ready to start.

Toby thought that he would have time to pay a
visit to his friends, the skeleton and the Fat Woman,

and to that end started toward the place where their tent had been standing. But to his sorrow he found that it was already being taken down, and he had only time to thank Mrs. Treat and to press the flesh-less hand of her shadowy husband as they entered their wagon to drive away.

He was disappointed, for he had hoped to be able to speak with his new-made friends a few moments before the weary night's ride commenced; but, fail-ing in that, he went hastily back to the monkey's cage. Old Ben was there, getting things ready for a start, but the wooden sides of the cage had not been put up and Toby had no difficulty in calling the aged monkey up to the bars. He held one of the Fat Woman's doughnuts in his hand and said, as he passed it through to the animal:

"I thought perhaps you might be hungry, Mr. Stubbs, and this is some of what the skeleton's wife give me. I hain't got very much time to talk with you now, but the first chance I can get away tomorrow, an' when there hain't anybody 'round, I want to tell you something."

The monkey had taken the doughnut in his hand-like paws and was tearing it to pieces, eating small portions of it very rapidly.

"Don't hurry yourself," said Toby warningly, "for Uncle Dan'l always told me the worst thing a feller could do was to eat fast. If you want any more before we start, just put your hand through the little hole up there near the seat, an' I'll give you all you want."

From the look on his face Toby confidently be-lieved the monkey was about to make some reply, but just then Ben shut up the sides, separating Toby and Mr. Stubbs, and the order was given to start.

Toby clambered up on to the high seat, Ben fol-lowed him, and in another instant the team was moving along slowly down the dusty road, preceded and followed by the many wagons, with their tiny, swinging lights.

"Well," said Ben, when he had got his team well under way and felt that he could indulge in a little conversation, "how did you get along today?"

Toby related all of his movements and gave the driver a faithful account of all that had happened to him, concluding his story by saying, "That was one of Mrs. Treat's doughnuts that I just gave to Mr. Stubbs."

"To whom?" asked Ben, in surprise.

"To Mr. Stubbs—the old fellow here in the cart, you know, that's been so good to me."

Toby heard a sort of gurgling sound, saw the driver's body sway back and forth in a trembling way, and was just becoming thoroughly alarmed, when he thought of the previous night and understood that Ben was only laughing in his own peculiar way.

"How did you know his name was Stubbs?" asked Ben, after he had recovered his breath.

"Oh, I don't know that that is his real name," was the quick reply, "I only call him that because he looks so much like a feller with that name that I knew at home. He don't seem to mind because I call him Stubbs."

Ben looked at Toby earnestly for a moment, acting all the time as if he wanted to laugh again, but didn't dare to, for fear he might burst a blood vessel; and then he said, as he patted him on the shoulder, "Well, you are the queerest little fish that I ever saw in all my travels. You seem to think that that monkey knows all you say to him."

"I'm sure he does," said Toby positively. "He don't say anything right out to me, but he knows everything I tell him. Do you suppose he could talk if he tried to?"

"Look here, Mr. Toby Tyler," and Ben turned half around in his seat and looked Toby full in the face, so as to give more emphasis to his words, "are you heathen enough to think that that monkey could talk if he wanted to?"

"I know I hain't a heathen," said Toby thoughtfully, "for if I had been some of the missionaries would have found me out a good while ago; but I never saw anybody like this old Mr. Stubbs before, an' I thought he could talk if he wanted to, just as the Living Skeleton does, or his wife. Anyhow, Mr. Stubbs winks at me; an' how could he do that if he didn't know what I've been sayin' to him?"

"Look here, my son," said Ben in a most fatherly fashion, "monkeys hain't anything but beasts, an' they don't know how to talk any more than they know what you say to 'em."

"Didn't you ever hear any of them speak a word?"

"Never. I've been in a circus, man an' boy, nigh on to forty years, an' I never seen nothin' in a monkey more'n any other beast, except their awful mischiefness."

"Well," said Toby, still unconvinced, "I believe Mr. Stubbs knows what I say to him, anyway."

"Now don't be foolish, Toby," pleaded Ben. "You can't show me one thing that a monkey ever did because you told him to."

Just at that moment, Toby felt someone pulling at the back of his coat and, looking round, he saw that it was a little brown hand reaching through the bars of the air hole of the cage, that was tugging away at his coat.

"There!" he said triumphantly to Ben. "Look there! I told Mr. Stubbs if he wanted anything more to eat, to tell me, an' I would give it to him. Now you can see for yourself that he's come for it." And Toby took a doughnut from his pocket and put it into the tiny hand, which was immediately withdrawn. "Now what do you think of Mr. Stubbs knowing what I say to him?"

"They often stick their paws up through there," said Ben, in a matter-of-fact tone. "I've had 'em pull my coat in the night till they made me as nervous as ever any old woman was. You see, Toby, my boy, monkeys is monkeys; an' you mustn't go to gettin' the idea that they're anything else, for it's a mistake. You think this old monkey in here knows what you say? Why, that's just the cuteness of the old fellow. He watches you to see if he can't do just as you do, an' that's all there is about it."

Toby was more than half convinced that Ben was putting the matter in its proper light, and he would have believed all that had been said if, just at that moment, he had not seen that brown hand reaching though the hole to clutch him again by the coat.

The action seemed so natural, so like a hungry boy who gropes in the dark pantry for something to eat, that it would have taken more arguments than Ben had at his disposal to persuade Toby that his Mr. Stubbs could not understand all that was said to him. Toby put another doughnut in the outstretched hand and then sat silently, as if in a brown study over some difficult problem.

For some time the ride was continued in silence. Ben was going through all the motions of whistling without uttering a sound—a favorite amusement of his—and Toby's thoughts were far away in the humble home he had scorned, with Uncle Daniel, whose virtues had increased in his esteem with every mile of distance which had been put between them, and whose faults had decreased in a corresponding ratio.

Toby's thoughtfulness had made him sleepy, and his eyes were almost closed in slumber, when he was startled by a crashing sound, was conscious of a feeling of being hurled from his seat by some great force, and then he lay senseless by the side of the road, while the wagon became a perfect wreck, from out of which a small army of monkeys was escaping. Ben's experienced ear had told him at the first crash that his wagon was breaking down, and, without having time to warn Toby of his peril, he had leaped clear of the wreck, keeping his horses under perfect control, and thus averting more trouble. It was the breaking of one of the axles which Toby had heard just before he was thrown from his seat and when the body of the wagon came down upon the hard road.

The monkeys, thus suddenly released from confinement, had scampered off in every direction, and by a singular chance, Toby's aged friend started for the woods in such a direction as to bring him directly before the boy's insensible form. The monkey, on coming up to Toby, stopped, urged by the well-known curiosity of its race, and began to examine the boy's person carefully, prying into pockets and trying to open the boy's half-closed eyelids. Fortunately for Toby, he had fallen upon a mud bank and was only stunned for the moment, having received no serious bruises. The attentions bestowed upon him by the monkey served the purpose of bringing him to his senses; and, after he had looked around him in the gray light of the coming morning, it would have taken far more of a philosopher than Old Ben was to persuade the boy that monkeys did not possess reasoning faculties.

The monkey was busy at Toby's ears, nose, and mouth, as monkeys will do when they get an opportunity, and the expression of its face was as grave as possible. Toby firmly believed that the monkey's face showed sorrow at his fall, and he imagined that the attentions which were bestowed upon him were for the purpose of learning whether he had been injured.

"Don't worry, Mr. Stubbs," said Toby, anxious to reassure his friend, as he sat upright and looked about him. "I didn't get hurt any; but I would like to know how I got 'way over here."

It really seemed as if the monkey was pleased to know that his little friend was not hurt, for he seated himself on his haunches, and his face expressed the liveliest pleasure that Toby was well again—or at least that was how the boy interpreted the look.

By this time the news of the accident had been shouted ahead from one team to the other, and all hands were hurrying to the scene for the purpose of rendering aid. As Toby saw them coming, he also saw a number of small forms, looking something like diminutive men, hurrying past him, and for the first time he understood how it was that the aged monkey was at liberty, and knew that those little dusky forms were the other occupants of the cage escaping to the woods.

"See there, Mr. Stubbs! See there!" he exclaimed, pointing toward the fugitives, "they're all going off into the woods! What shall we do?"

The sight of the runaways seemed to excite the old monkey quite as much as it did the boy. He sprang to his feet, chattering in the most excited way, screamed two or three times, as if he were calling them back, and then started off in vigorous pursuit.

"Now he's gone, too!" said Toby disconsolately, believing that the old fellow had run away from him. "I didn't think Mr. Stubbs would treat me this way!"

[8]

Capture of the Monkeys

THE BOY tried to rise to his feet, but his head whirled so, and he felt so dizzy and sick from the effects of his fall, that he was obliged to sit down again until he should feel able to stand. Meanwhile the crowd around the wagon paid no attention to him, and he lay there quietly enough, until he heard the hateful voice of Mr. Lord, asking if his boy were hurt.

The sound of his voice affected Toby very much as the chills and fever affect a sufferer, and he shook so with fear, and his heart beat so loudly, that he thought Mr. Lord must know where he was by the sound. Seeing, however, that his employer did not come directly toward him, the thought flashed upon his mind that now would be a good chance to run away, and he acted upon it at once. He rolled himself over in the mud until he reached a low growth of fir trees that skirted the road, and when beneath their friendly shade, he arose to his feet and walked swiftly toward the woods, following the direction the monkeys had taken.

He no longer felt dizzy and sick: the fear of Mr. Lord had dispelled all that, and he felt strong and active again.

He had walked rapidly for some distance and was nearly beyond the sound of the voices in the road, when he was startled by seeing quite a procession of figures emerge from the trees and come directly toward him.

He could not understand the meaning of this strange company, and it so frightened him that he attempted to hide behind a tree, in the hope that they might pass without seeing him. But no sooner had he secreted himself than a strange, shrill chattering came from the foremost of the group, and in an instant Toby emerged from his place of concealment.

He had recognized the peculiar sound as that of the old monkey who had left him a few moments before, and he knew now what he did not know then, owing to the darkness. The newcomers were the monkeys that had escaped from the cage and had been overtaken and compelled to come back by the old monkey, who seemed to have the most perfect control over them.

The old fellow was leading the band, and all were linked "hand in hand" with each other, which gave the whole crowd a most comical appearance as they came up to Toby, half hopping, half walking upright, and all chattering and screaming like a crowd of children out for a holiday.

Toby stepped toward the noisy crowd, held out his hand gravely to the old monkey, and said, in tones of heartfelt sorrow: "I felt awful bad because I thought you had gone off an' left me, when you only went off to find the other fellows. You're awful good, Mr. Stubbs, an' now, instead of runnin' away, as I was goin' to do, we'll all go back together."

The old monkey grasped Toby's extended hand with his disengaged paw and, clinging firmly to it, the whole crowd followed in unbroken line, chattering and scolding at the most furious rate, while every now and then Mr. Stubbs would look back and scream out something, which would cause the confusion to cease for an instant.

It was really a comical sight, but Toby seemed to think it the most natural thing in the world that they should follow him in this manner, and he chattered to the old monkey quite as fast as any of the others were doing. He told him very gravely all that he knew about the accident, explained why it was that he conceived the idea of running away, and really believed that Mr. Stubbs understood every word he was saying.

Very shortly after Toby had started to run away, the proprietor of the circus drove up to the scene of disaster; and, after seeing that the wagon was being rapidly fixed up so that it could be hauled to the next town, he ordered that search should be made for the monkeys. It was very important that they should be captured at once, and he appeared to think more of the loss of the animals than of the damage done to the wagon.

While the men were forming a plan for a search for the truants, so that in case of a capture they could let each other know, the noise made by Toby and his party was heard, and the men stood still to learn what it meant.

The entire party burst into shouts of laughter as Toby and his companions walked into the circle of light formed by the glare of the lanterns, and the merriment was by no means abated at Toby's serious demeanor. The wagon was now standing upright, with the door open, and Toby therefore led his com-

The old monkey grasped Toby's hand, and the whole crowd followed in unbroken line

panions directly to it, gravely motioning them to enter.

The old monkey, instead of obeying, stepped back to Toby's side and screamed to the others in such a manner that they all entered the cage, leaving him on the outside with the boy.

Toby motioned him to get in, too, but he clung to his hand and scolded so furiously that it was apparent he had no idea of leaving his boy companion. One of the men stepped up and was about to force him into the wagon, when the proprietor ordered him to stop.

"What boy is that?" he asked.

"Job Lord's new boy," said someone in the crowd.

The man asked Toby how it was that he had succeeded in capturing all the runaways, and he answered gravely:

"Mr. Stubbs an' I are good friends, an' when he saw the others runnin' away, he just stopped 'em an' brought 'em back to me. I wish you'd let Mr. Stubbs ride with me; we like each other a good deal."

"You can do just what you please with Mr. Stubbs, as you call him. I expected to lose half the monkeys in that cage, and you have brought back every one. That monkey shall be yours, and you may put him in the cage whenever you want to or take him with you, just as you choose, for he belongs entirely to you."

Toby's joy knew no bounds; he put his arm around the monkey's neck, and the monkey clung firmly to him, until even Job Lord was touched at the evidence of affection between the two.

While the wagon was being repaired, Toby and the monkey stood hand in hand watching the work go on, while those in the cage scolded and raved because they had been induced to return to captivity. After a while the old monkey seated himself on

Toby's arm and cuddled close up to him, uttering now and then a contented sort of little squeak as the boy talked to him.

That night Mr. Stubbs slept in Toby's arms, in the bandwagon, and both boy and monkey appeared very well contented with their lot, which a short time previous had seemed so hard.

When Toby awakened to his second day's work with the circus, his monkey friend was seated by his side, gravely exploring his pockets, and all the boy's treasures were being spread out on the floor of the wagon by his side. Toby remonstrated with him on this breach of confidence, but Mr. Stubbs was more in the mood for sport than for grave conversation, and the more Toby talked, the more mischievous did he become, until at length the boy gathered up his little store of treasures, took the monkey by the paw, and walked him toward the cage from which he had escaped on the previous night.

"Now, Mr. Stubbs," said Toby, speaking in an injured tone, "you must go in here and stay till I have got more time to fool with you."

He opened the door of the cage, but the monkey struggled as well as he was able, and Toby was obliged to exert all his strength to put him in.

When once the door was fastened upon him, Toby tried to impress upon his monkey friend's mind the importance of being more sedate, and he was convinced that the words had sunk deep into Mr. Stubbs's heart, for, by the time he had concluded, the old monkey was seated in the corner of the cage, looking up from under his shaggy eyebrows in the most reproachful manner possible.

Toby felt sorry that he had spoken so harshly and was about to make amends for his severity, when Mr. Lord's gruff voice recalled him to the fact that his time was not his own, and he therefore commenced his day's work, but with a lighter heart than he had had since he stole away from Uncle Daniel and Guilford.

This day was not very much different from the preceding one so far as the manner of Mr. Lord and his partner toward the boy was concerned. They seemed to have an idea that he was doing only about half as much work as he ought to, and both united in swearing at and abusing him as much as possible.

As far as his relations with other members of the company were concerned, Toby now stood in a much better position than before. Those who had witnessed the scene told the others how Toby had led in the monkeys on the night previous, and nearly every member of the company had a kind word for the little fellow whose head could hardly be seen above the counter of Messrs. Lord and Jacobs' booth.

[9]

The Dinner Party

AT NOON Toby was thoroughly tired out, for whenever anyone spoke kindly to him, Mr. Lord seemed
to take a malicious pleasure in giving him extra tasks
to do, until Toby began to hope that no one else
would pay any attention to him. On this day he was
permitted to go to dinner first, and after he returned,
he was left in charge of the booth. Trade being dull,
as it usually was during the dinner hour, he had very
little work to do after he had cleaned the glasses
and set things to rights generally.

When, therefore, he saw the gaunt form of the
skeleton emerge from his tent and come toward him
he was particularly pleased, for he had begun to
think very kindly of the thin man and his fleshy wife.

"Well, Toby," said the skeleton, as he came up to
the booth, carefully dusted Mr. Lord's private chair,
and sat down very cautiously in it, as if he expected
it would break down under his weight, "I hear you've
been making quite a hero of yourself by capturing
the monkeys last night."

Toby's freckled face reddened with pleasure as he heard these words and he stammered out with considerable difficulty, "I didn't do anything; it was Mr. Stubbs that brought 'em back."

"Mr. Stubbs!" And the skeleton laughed so heartily that Toby was afraid he would dislocate some of his thinly covered joints. "When you was tellin' about Mr. Stubbs yesterday, I thought you meant someone belonging to the company. You ought to have seen my wife Lilly shake with laughing when I told her who Mr. Stubbs was!"

"Yes," said Toby, at a loss to know just what to say, "I should think she *would* shake when she laughs."

"She does," replied the skeleton. "If you could see her when something funny strikes her, you'd think she was one of those big plates of jelly that they have in the bakeshop windows." And Mr. Treat looked proudly at the gaudy picture which represented his wife in all her monstrosity of flesh. "She's a great woman, Toby, an' she's got a great head."

Toby nodded his head in assent. He would have liked to have said something nice regarding Mrs. Treat, but he really did not know what to say, so he simply contented himself and the fond husband by nodding.

"She thinks a good deal of you, Toby," continued the skeleton, as he moved his chair to a position more favorable for him to elevate his feet on the edge of the counter, and placed his handkerchief under him as a cushion, "she's talking of you all the time, and if you wasn't such a little fellow I should begin to be jealous of you—I should, upon my word."

"You're—both—very—good," stammered Toby, so weighted down by a sense of the honor heaped upon him as to be at a loss for words.

"An' she wants to see more of you. She made me

come out here now, when she knew Mr. Lord would be away, to tell you that we're goin' to have a little kind of a friendly dinner in our tent tomorrow—she's cooked it all herself, or she's going to—and we want you to come in an' have some with us."

Toby's eyes glistened at the thought of the unexpected pleasure, and then his face grew sad as he replied, "I'd like to come first-rate, Mr. Treat, but I don't s'pose Mr. Lord would let me stay away from the shop long enough."

"Why, you won't have any work to do tomorrow, Toby—it's Sunday."

"So it is!" said the boy, with a pleased smile, as he thought of the day of rest which was so near. And then he added quickly, "An' this is Saturday afternoon. What fun the boys at home are havin'! You see there hain't any school Saturday afternoons, an' all the fellers go out in the woods."

"And you wish you were there to go with them, don't you?" asked the skeleton sympathetically.

"Indeed I do!" exclaimed Toby quickly. "It's twice as good as any circus that ever was."

"But you didn't think so before you came with us, did you?"

"I didn't know so much about circuses then as I do now," replied the boy sadly.

Mr. Treat saw that he was touching on a sore subject and one which was arousing sad thoughts in his little companion's mind, and he hastened to change it at once.

"Then I can tell Lilly that you'll come, can I?"

"Oh, yes, I'll be sure to be there; an' I want you to know just how good I think you both are to me."

"That's all right, Toby," said Mr. Treat, with a pleased expression on his face, "an' you may bring Mr. Stubbs with you, if you want to."

"Thank you," said Toby, "I'm sure Mr. Stubbs will be just as glad to come as I shall. But where will we be tomorrow?"

"Right here. We always stay over Sunday at the place where we show Saturday. But I must be going, or Lilly will worry her life out of her for fear I'm somewhere getting cold. She's awful careful of me, that woman is. You'll be on hand tomorrow at one o'clock, won't you?"

"Indeed I will," said Toby emphatically, "an' I'll bring Mr. Stubbs with me, too."

With a friendly nod of the head, the skeleton hurried away to reassure his wife that he was safe and well. And before he had hardly disappeared within the tent, Toby had another caller, who was none other than his friend Old Ben, the driver.

"Well, my boy," shouted Ben in his cheery, hearty tones, "I haven't seen you since you left the wagon so sudden last night. Did you get shook up much?"

"Oh, no," replied Toby, "you see I hain't very big, an' then I struck in the mud; so I got off pretty easy."

"That's a fact; an' you can thank your lucky stars for it, too, for I've seen grown-up men get pitched off a wagon in that way an' break their necks doin' it. But has Job told you where you was going to sleep tonight? You know we stay over here till tomorrow."

"I didn't think anything about that; but I s'pose I'll sleep in the wagon, won't I?"

"You can sleep at the hotel, if you want to; but the beds will likely be dirty. An' if you take my advice, you'll crawl into some of the wagons in the tent."

Ben then explained to him that, after his work was done that night, he would not be expected to report for duty until the time for starting on Sunday night, and concluded his remarks by saying:

"Now you know what your rights are, an' don't

you let Job impose on you in any way. I'll be round here after you get through work, an' we'll bunk in somewhere together."

The arrival of Messrs. Lord and Jacobs put a stop to the conversation and was the signal for Toby's time of trial. It seemed to him, and with good reason, that the chief delight these men had in life was to torment him, for neither ever spoke a pleasant word to him. And when one was not giving him some difficult work to do or finding fault in some way, the other would be sure to do so; and Toby had very little comfort from the time he began work in the morning until he stopped at night.

It was not until after the evening performance was over that Toby had a chance to speak with Mr. Stubbs, and then he was so tired that he simply took the old monkey from the cage, nestled him under his jacket, and lay down with him to sleep in the place which Old Ben had selected.

When the morning came, Mr. Stubbs aroused his young master at a much earlier hour than he would have awakened had he been left to himself, and the two went out for a short walk before breakfast. They went instinctively toward the woods; and when the shade of the trees was once reached, how the two reveled in their feedom! Mr. Stubbs climbed into the trees, swung himself from one to the other by means of his tail, gathered half-ripe nuts, which he threw at his master, tried to catch the birds, and had a good time generally.

Toby, stretched at full length on the mossy bank, watched the antics of his pet, laughing boisterously at times as Mr. Stubbs would do some one thing more comical than usual, and forgot there was in this world such a thing as a circus or such a man as Job Lord. It was to Toby a morning without a flaw, and he took no heed of the time, until the sound of the church bells warned him of the lateness of the hour, reminding him at the same time of where he should be—where he would be, if he were at home with Uncle Daniel.

In the meantime the old monkey had been trying to attract his young master's attention, and, failing in his efforts, he came down from the tree, crept softly up to Toby, and nestled his head under the boy's arm.

This little act of devotion seemed to cause Toby's grief to burst forth afresh, and clasping the monkey around the neck, hugging him close to his bosom, he sobbed:

"Oh, Mr. Stubbs, Mr. Stubbs, how lonesome we are! If we was only at Uncle Dan'l's, we'd be the two happiest people in all this world. We could play on the hay or go up to the pasture or go down to the village; an' I'd work my fingers off if I could only be there just once more. It was wicked for me to run away, an' now I'm gettin' paid for it."

He hugged the monkey closely, swaying his body to and fro, and presenting a perfect picture of grief. The monkey, not knowing what to make of this changed mood, cowered whimperingly in his arms, looking up into his face and licking the boy's hands whenever he had the opportunity.

It was some time before Toby's grief exhausted itself; and then, still clasping the monkey, he hurried out of the woods toward the town and the now thoroughly hated circus tents.

The clocks were just striking one as Toby entered the enclosure used by the show as a place of performance, and, remembering his engagement with the skeleton and his wife, he went directly to their tent. From the odors which assailed him as he entered, it was very evident that a feast of no mean proportions was in course of preparation and Toby's keen appetite returned in full vigor. Even the monkey seemed affected by the odor, for he danced about on his master's shoulder and chattered so that Toby was obliged to choke him a little in order to make him present a respectable appearance.

When Toby reached the interior of the tent, he was astonished at the extent of the preparations that were being made, and gazed around him in surprise. The platform on which the lean man and fat woman were in the habit of exhibiting themselves now bore a long table loaded with eatables; and, from the fact that eight or ten chairs were ranged around it, Toby understood that he was not the only guest invited to the feast. Some little attempt had also been made at decoration by festooning the end of the tent where the platform was placed with two or three flags and some streamers, and the tent poles also were fringed with tissue paper of the brightest colors.

Toby had only time enough to notice this when the skeleton advanced toward him, and, with the liveliest appearance of pleasure, said, as he took him by the hands with a grip that made him wince:

"It gives me great joy, Mr. Tyler, to welcome you at one of our little home reunions, if one can call a tent, that is moved every day in the week, home."

Toby hardly knew whom Mr. Treat referred to when he said, "Mr. Tyler," but by the time his hands were released from the bony grasp, he understood that it was himself who was spoken to.

The skeleton then formally introduced him to the other guests present, who were sitting at one end of the tent and evidently anxiously awaiting the coming feast.

"These," said Mr. Treat, as he waved his hand

toward two white-haired, pink-eyed young ladies, who sat with their arms twined around each other's waist, and had been eying the monkey with some appearance of fear, "are the Miss Cushings, known to the world as the Albino Children. They command a large salary and form a very attractive feature of our exhibition."

The young ladies arose at the same time, as if they had been the Siamese Twins and could not act independently of each other, and bowed.

Toby made the best bow he was capable of, and the monkey made frantic efforts to escape, as if he would enjoy twisting his paws in their perpendicular hair.

"And this," continued Mr. Treat, pointing to a sickly, sour-looking individual, who was sitting apart from the others, with his arms folded, and looking as if he was counting the very seconds before the dinner should begin, "is the wonderful Signor Castro, whose sword-swallowing feats you have doubtless heard of."

Toby stepped back just one step, as if overwhelmed by awe at beholding the signor in the guise of a humble individual; and the gentleman who gained his livelihood by swallowing swords unbent his dignity so far as to unfold his arms and present a very dirty-looking hand for Toby to shake. The boy took hold of the outstretched hand, wondering why the signor never used soap and water, and Mr. Stubbs, apparently afraid of the sour-looking man, retreated to Toby's shoulder, where he sat chattering and scolding about the introduction.

Again the skeleton waved his hand, and this time he introduced "Mademoiselle Spelletti, the wonderful snake charmer, whose exploits in this country and before the crowned heads of Europe had caused

[72]

the whole world to stand aghast at her daring."

Mademoiselle Spelletti was a very ordinary-looking young lady of about twenty-five years of age, who looked very much as if her name might originally have been Murphy, and she too extended a hand for Toby to grasp—only her hand was clean, and she appeared to be a very much more pleasant acquaintance than the gentleman who swallowed swords.

This ended the introductions, and Toby was just looking around for a seat, when Mrs. Treat, the fat lady, and the giver of the feast which was about to come and which already smelled so invitingly, entered from behind a curtain of canvas, where the cooking stove was supposed to be located.

She had every appearance of being the cook for the occasion. Her sleeves were rolled up, her hair tumbled and frowzy, and there were several unmistakable marks of grease on the front of her calico dress.

She waited for no ceremony, but rushed up to Toby and, taking him in her arms, gave him such a squeeze that there seemed to be every possibility that she would break all the bones in his body. And she kept him so long in this bearlike embrace that Mr. Stubbs reached his little brown paws over and got such a hold of her hair that all present, save Signor Castro, rushed forward to release her from the monkey's grasp.

"You dear little thing!" said Mrs. Treat, paying but slight attention to the hair pulling she had just undergone and holding Toby at arm's length, so that she could look into his face, "you were so late that I was afraid you wasn't coming, and my dinner wouldn't have tasted half so good if you hadn't been here to eat some."

Toby hardly knew what to say for this hearty wel-

Toby hardly knew what to say for this hearty welcome

come, but he managed to tell the large and kind-hearted lady that he had had no idea of missing the dinner and that he was very glad she wanted him to come.

"Want you to come, you dear little thing!" she exclaimed, as she gave him another hug, but careful not to give Mr. Stubbs a chance of grasping her hair again. "Of course I wanted you to come, for this dinner has been got up so that you could meet these people here, and so that they could see you."

Toby was entirely at a loss to know what to say to this overwhelming compliment, and for that reason did not say anything, only submitting impatiently to the third hug, which was all Mrs. Treat had time to give him, for she was obliged to run behind the canvas screen again, as there were unmistakable sounds of something boiling over on the stove.

"You'll excuse me," said the skeleton, with an air of dignity, waving his hand once more toward the assembled company, "but, while introducing you to Mr. Tyler, I had almost forgotten to introduce him to you. This, ladies and gentlemen"—and here he touched Toby on the shoulder, as if he were some living curiosity whose habits and mode of capture he was about to explain to a party of spectators—"is Mr. Toby Tyler, of whom you heard on the night when the monkey cage was smashed, and who now carries with him the identical monkey which was presented to him by the manager of this great show as a token of esteem for his skill and bravery in capturing the entire lot of monkeys without a single blow."

By the time that Mr. Treat got through with this long speech Toby felt very much as if he were some wonderful creature whom the skeleton was exhibiting; but he managed to rise to his feet and duck his little red head in his best imitation of a bow. Then he sat down and hugged Mr. Stubbs to cover his confusion.

One of the Albino Children now came forward and, while stroking Mr. Stubbs's hair, looked so intently at Toby that for the life of him he couldn't say which she regarded as the curiosity, himself or the monkey. Therefore he hastened to say, modestly:

"I didn't do much toward catchin' the monkeys; Mr. Stubbs here did almost all of it, an' I only led 'em in."

"There, there, my boy," said the skeleton in a fatherly tone, "I've heard the whole story from Old Ben, an' I sha'n't let you get out of it like that. We all know what you did, an' it's no use for you to deny any part of it."

[10]

Mr. Stubbs at a Party

TOBY WAS about to say that he did not intend to represent the matter other than it really was, when a voice from behind the canvas screen arrested further conversation.

"Sam-u-el, come an' help me carry these things in."

Something very like a smile of satisfaction passed over Signor Castro's face as he heard this, which told him that the time for the feast was near at hand; and the snake charmer, as well as the Albino Children, seemed quite as much pleased as did the sword swallower.

"You will excuse me, ladies and gentlemen," said the skeleton in an important tone, "I must help Lilly, and then I shall have the pleasure of helping you to some of her cooking, which, if I do say it, that oughtn't, is as good as can be found in this entire country."

Then he, too, disappeared behind the canvas screen.

Left alone, Toby looked at the ladies, and the

ladies looked at him, in perfect silence, while the sword swallower grimly regarded them all, until Mr. Treat reappeared, bearing on a platter an immense turkey, as nicely browned as any Thanksgiving turkey Toby ever saw. Behind him came his fat wife, carrying several dishes, each of which emitted a most fragrant odor. And as these were placed upon the table the spirits of the sword swallower seemed to revive, and he smiled pleasantly; while even the ladies appeared animated by the sight and odor of the good things which they were to be called upon so soon to pass judgment.

Several times did Mr. and Mrs. Treat bustle in and out from behind the screen, and each time they made some addition to that which was upon the table, until Toby feared they would never finish, and the sword swallower seemed unable to restrain his impatience.

At last the finishing touch had been put to the table, the last dish placed in position, and then, with a certain kind of grace, which no one but a man as thin as Mr. Treat could assume, he advanced to the edge of the platform and said:

"Ladies and gentlemen, nothing gives me greater pleasure than to invite you all, including Mr. Tyler's friend Stubbs, to the bountiful repast which my Lilly has prepared for—"

At this point, Mr. Treat's speech—for it certainly seemed as if he had commenced to make one—was broken off in a most summary manner. His wife had come up behind him, and, with as much ease as if he had been a child, lifted him from off the floor and placed him gently in the chair at the head of the table.

"Come right up and get dinner," she said to her guests. "If you had waited until Samuel had finished his speech, everything on the table would have been stone cold."

The guests proceeded to obey her kindly command; and it is to be regretted that the sword swallower had no better manners than to jump on to the platform with one bound and seat himself at the table with the most unseemly haste. The others, and more especially Toby, proceeded in a leisurely and more dignified manner.

A seat had been placed by the side of the one intended for Toby for the accommodation of Mr. Stubbs, who suffered a napkin to be tied under his chin and behaved generally in a manner that gladdened the heart of his young master.

Mr. Treat cut generous slices from the turkey for each guest, and Mrs. Treat piled their plates high with all sorts of vegetables, complaining, after the manner of housewives generally, that the food was not cooked as she would like to have had it, and declaring that she had had poor luck with everything that morning, when she firmly believed in her heart that her table had never looked better.

After the company had had the edge taken off their appetites—which effect was produced on the sword swallower only after he had been helped three different times, the conversation began by the Fat Woman asking Toby how he got along with Mr. Lord.

Toby could not give a very good account of his employer, but he had the good sense not to cast a damper on a party of pleasure by reciting his own troubles; so he said evasively:

"I guess I shall get along pretty well, now that I have got so many friends."

Just as he had commenced to speak, the skeleton had put into his mouth a very large piece of turkey—

very much larger in proportion than himself—and when Toby had finished speaking, he started to say something evidently not very complimentary to Mr. Lord. But what it was the company never knew; for just as he opened his mouth to speak, the food went down the wrong way, his face became a bright purple, and it was quite evident that he was choking.

Toby was alarmed and sprang from his chair to assist his friend, upsetting Mr. Stubbs from his seat, causing him to scamper up the tent pole, with the napkin still tied around his neck, and to scold in his most vehement manner. Before Toby could reach the skeleton, however, the Fat Woman had darted toward her lean husband, caught him by the arm, and was pounding his back, by the time Toby got there, so vigorously that the boy was afraid her enormous hand would go through his tissue-paper-like frame.

"I wouldn't," said Toby in alarm, "you may break him."

"Don't you get frightened," said Mrs. Treat, turning her husband completely over and still continuing the drumming process. "He's often taken this way; he's such a glutton that he'd try to swallow the turkey whole if he could get it in his mouth, an' he's so thin that 'most anything sticks in his throat."

"I should think you'd break him all up," said Toby apologetically, as he resumed his seat at the table. "He don't look as if he could stand very much of that sort of thing."

But apparently Mr. Treat could stand very much more than Toby gave him credit for, because at this juncture he stopped coughing, and his face fast assumed its natural hue.

His attentive wife, seeing that he had ceased struggling, lifted him in her arms, and sat him down in his chair with a force that threatened to snap his very head off.

"There!" she said, as he wheezed a little from the effects of the shock, "now see if you can behave yourself, an' chew your meat as you ought to! One of these days when you're alone you'll try that game, and that'll be the last of you."

"If he'd try to do one of my tricks long enough, he'd get so that there wouldn't hardly anything choke him," the sword swallower ventured to suggest mildly, as he wiped a small stream of cranberry sauce from his chin and laid a well-polished turkey bone by the side of his plate.

"I'd like to see him try it!" said the fat lady, with just a shade of anger in her voice. Then turning toward her husband, she said emphatically, "Samuel, don't you ever let me catch *you* swallowing a sword!"

"I won't, my love, I won't; and I will try to chew my meat more," replied the very thin glutton, in a feeble tone.

Toby thought that perhaps the skeleton might keep the first part of that promise, but he was not quite sure about the last.

It required no little coaxing on the part of both Toby and Mrs. Treat to induce Mr. Stubbs to come down from his lofty perch. But the task was accomplished at last, and by the gift of a very large doughnut he was induced to resume his seat at the table.

The time had now come when the duties of a host, in his own peculiar way of viewing them, devolved upon Mr. Treat, and he said, as he pushed his chair back a short distance from the table and tried to polish the front of his vest with his napkin:

"I don't want this fact lost sight of, because it is an important one: everyone must remember that we gathered here to meet and become better acquainted with the latest and best addition to this circus, Mr. Toby Tyler."

Poor Toby! As the company all looked directly at him, and Mrs. Treat nodded her enormous head energetically, as if to say that she agreed exactly with her husband, the poor boy's face grew very red and the squash pie lost its flavor.

"Although Mr. Tyler may not be exactly one of us, owing to the fact that he does not belong to the profession, but is only one of the adjuncts to it, so to speak," continued the skeleton, in a voice which was fast being raised to its highest pitch, "we feel proud, after his exploits at the time of the accident, to have him with us, and gladly welcome him now, through the medium of this little feast prepared by my Lilly."

Here the Albino Children nodded their heads in approval, and the sword swallower gave a grunt of assent. Thus encouraged, the skeleton proceeded:

"I feel, when I say that we like and admire Mr. Tyler, all present will agree with me, and all would like to hear him say a word for himself."

The skeleton seemed to have expressed the views of those present remarkably well, judging from their expressions of pleasure and assent, and all waited for the honored guest to speak.

Toby knew that he must say something, but he couldn't think of a single thing. He tried over and over again to call to his mind something which he had read as to how people acted and what they said when they were expected to speak at a dinner table, but his thoughts refused to go back for him, and the silence was actually becoming painful. Finally, and with the greatest effort, he managed to say, with a very perceptible stammer, and while his face was growing very red:

"I know I ought to say something to pay for this big dinner that you said was gotten up for me, but I don't know what to say, unless to thank you for it. You see I hain't big enough to say much, an', as Uncle Dan'l says, I don't amount to very much 'cept for eatin', an' I guess he's right. You're all real good to me, an' when I get to be a man, I'll try to do as much for you."

Toby had risen to his feet when he began to make his speech, and while he was speaking, Mr. Stubbs had crawled over into his chair. When he finished, he sat down again without looking behind him and of course sat plump on the monkey. There was a loud outcry from Mr. Stubbs, a little frightened noise from Toby, an instant's scrambling, and then boy, monkey, and chair tumbled off the platform, landing on the ground in an indescribable mass, from which the monkey extricated himself more quickly than Toby could, and again took refuge on the top of the tent pole.

Of course all the guests ran to Toby's assistance, and while the Fat Woman poked him all over to see that none of his bones were broken, the skeleton brushed the dirt from his clothes.

All this time the monkey screamed, yelled, and danced around on the tent pole and ropes as if his feelings had received a shock from which he could never recover.

"I didn't mean to end it up that way, but it was Mr. Stubbs's fault," said Toby, as soon as quiet had been restored, and the guests, with the exception of the monkey, were seated at the table once more.

"Of course you didn't," said Mrs. Treat, in a kindly tone. "But don't you feel bad about it one bit, for you ought to thank your lucky stars that you didn't break any of your bones."

"I s'pose I did," said Toby soberly, as he looked back at the scene of his disaster and then up at the chattering monkey that had caused all the trouble.

Shortly after this, Mr. Stubbs having again been coaxed down from his lofty position, Toby took his departure, promising to call as often during the week as he could get away from his exacting employers.

Just outside the tent he met Old Ben, who said, as he showed signs of indulging in another of his internal laughing spells:

"Hello! Has the skeleton an' his lily of a wife been givin' a blowout to you, too?"

"They invited me in there to dinner," said Toby modestly.

"Of course they did—of course they did," replied Ben with a chuckle. "They carries a cookin' stove along with 'em, so's they can give these little spreads whenever we stay over a day in a place. Oh, I've been there!"

"And did they ask you to make a speech?"

"Of course. Did they try it on you?"

"Yes," said Toby mournfully, "an' I tumbled off the platform when I got through."

"I didn't do exactly that," replied Ben thoughtfully, "but I s'pose you got too much steam on, seein' 's how it was likely your first speech. Now, you'd better go into the tent an' try to get a little sleep, 'cause we've got a long ride tonight over a rough road, an' you won't get more'n a cat nap all night."

"But where are you going?" asked Toby, as he shifted Mr. Stubbs over to his other shoulder, preparatory to following his friend's advice.

"I'm goin' to church," said Ben, and then Toby noticed for the first time that the old driver had made some attempt at dressing up. "I've been with the circus, man an' boy, for nigh to forty years, an' I allus go to meetin' once on Sunday. It's somethin' I promised my old mother I would do, an' I hain't broke my promise yet."

"Why don't you take me with you?" asked Toby, wistfully, as he thought of the little church on the hill at home, and wished—oh, so earnestly!—that he was there then, even at the risk of being thumped on the head with Uncle Daniel's book.

"If I'd seen you this mornin', I would," said Ben, "but now you must try to bottle up some sleep agin tonight, an' next Sunday I'll take you."

With these words Old Ben started off, and Toby proceeded to carry out his wishes, although he rather doubted the possibility of "bottling up" any sleep that afternoon.

He lay down on the top of the wagon, after having put Mr. Stubbs inside with the others of his tribe, and in a very few moments the boy was sound asleep, dreaming of a dinner party at which Mr. Stubbs made a speech and he himself scampered up and down the tent pole.

[11]

A Stormy Night

WHEN TOBY awoke, it was nearly dark, and the bustle around him told very plainly that the time for departure was near at hand. He rubbed his eyes just enough to make sure that he was thoroughly awake and then jumped down from his rather lofty bed and ran around to the door of the cage to assure himself that Mr. Stubbs was safe. This done, his preparations for the journey were made.

Now Toby noticed that each one of the drivers was clad in rubber clothing, and, after listening for a moment, he learned the cause of their waterproof garments. It was raining very hard, and Toby thought with dismay of the long ride that he would have to take on the top of the monkey's cage, with no protection whatever save that afforded by his ordinary clothing.

While he was standing by the side of the wagon, wondering how he should get along, Old Ben came in. The water was pouring from his clothes in little rivulets, and he offered most unmistakable evidence of the damp state of the weather. "It's a nasty night, my boy," said the old driver, in much the same cheery tone that he would have used had he been informing Toby that it was a beautiful moonlight evening.

"I guess I'll get wet," said Toby ruefully, as he looked up at the lofty seat which he was to occupy.

"Bless me!" said Ben, as if the thought had just come to him, "it won't do for you to ride outside on a night like this. Wait here, an' I'll see what I can do for you."

The old man hurried off to the other end of the tent, and almost before Toby thought he had time to go as far as the ring he returned.

"It's all right," he said, and this time in a gruff voice, as if he were announcing some misfortune, "you're to ride in the women's wagon. Come with me."

Toby followed without a question, though he was wholly at a loss to understand what the "women's wagon" was, for he had never seen anything which looked like one.

He soon learned, however, when Old Ben stopped in front—or, rather, at the end—of a long, covered wagon that looked like an omnibus, except that it was considerably longer, and the seats inside were divided by arms, padded, to make them comfortable to lean against.

"Here's the boy," said Ben, as he lifted Toby up on the step, gave him a gentle push to intimate that he was to get inside, and then left him.

As Toby stepped inside, he saw that the wagon was nearly full of women and children. And fearing lest he should take a seat that belonged to someone else, he stood in the middle of the wagon, not knowing what to do.

"Why don't you sit down, little boy?" asked one of

the ladies, after Toby had remained standing nearly five minutes and the wagon was about to start.

"Well," said Toby, with some hesitation, as he looked around at the two or three empty seats that remained, "I didn't want to get in anybody else's place, an' I didn't know where to sit."

"Come right here," said the lady, as she pointed to a seat by the side of a little girl who did not look any older than Toby, "the lady who usually occupies that seat will not be here tonight, and you can have it."

"Thank you, ma'am," said Toby, as he sat timidly down on the edge of the seat, hardly daring to sit back comfortably and feeling very awkward meanwhile, but congratulating himself on being thus protected from the pouring rain.

The wagon started, and as each one talked with her neighbor, Toby felt a most dismal sense of loneliness and almost wished that he was riding on the monkey cart with Ben, where he could have someone to talk with. He gradually pushed himself back into a more comfortable position and had then an opportunity of seeing more plainly the young girl who rode by his side.

She was quite as young as Toby and small of her age; but there was an old look about her face that made the boy think of her as being an old woman cut down to fit children's clothes. Toby had looked at her so earnestly that she observed him, and asked, "What is your name?"

"Toby Tyler."

"What do you do in the circus?"

"Sell candy for Mr. Lord."

"Oh! I thought you was a new member of the company."

Toby knew by the tone of her voice that he had fallen considerably in her estimation by not being one of the performers, and it was some little time before he ventured to speak. And then he asked timidly, "What do you do?"

"I ride one of the horses with mother."

"Are you the little girl that comes out with the lady an' four horses?" asked Toby, in awe that he should be conversing with so famous a person.

"Yes, I am. Don't I do it nicely?"

"Why, you're a perfect little—little—fairy!" exclaimed Toby, after hesitating a moment to find some word which would exactly express his idea.

This praise seemed to please the young lady, and in a short time the two became very good friends, even if Toby did not occupy a more exalted position than that of candy seller. She had learned from him all about the accident to the monkey cage and about Mr. Stubbs, and in return had told him that her name was Ella Mason, though on the bills she was called, "Mademoiselle Jeannette."

For a long time the two children sat talking together, and then Mademoiselle Jeannette curled herself up on the seat, with her head in her mother's lap, and went to sleep.

Toby had resolved to keep awake and watch her, for he was struck with admiration at her face; but sleep got the better of him in less than five minutes after he had made the resolution, and he sat bolt upright, with his little round head nodding and bobbing until it seemed almost certain that he would shake it off.

When Toby awoke, the wagon was drawn up by the side of the road, the sun was shining brightly, preparations were being made for the entrée into town, and the harsh voice of Mr. Job Lord was shouting his name in a tone that boded no good for poor Toby when he should make his appearance.

*"Are you the little girl that comes out with the lady
and four horses?" asked Toby*

Toby would have hesitated before meeting his angry employer but that he knew it would only make matters worse for him when he did show himself, and he mentally braced himself for the trouble which he knew was coming. The little girl whose acquaintance he had made the night previous was still sleeping. And wishing to say good-by to her in some way without awakening her, he stooped down and gently kissed the skirt of her dress. Then he went out to meet his master.

Mr. Lord was thoroughly enraged when Toby left the wagon and saw the boy just as he stepped to the ground. The angry man gave a quick glance around, to make sure that none of Toby's friends were in sight, and then caught him by the coat collar and commenced to whip him severely with the small rubber cane that he usually carried.

Mr. Job Lord lifted the poor boy entirely clear of the ground, and each blow that he struck could be heard almost the entire length of the circus train.

"You've been makin' so many acquaintances here that you hain't willin' to do any work," he said, savagely, as he redoubled the force of his blows.

"Oh, please stop! Please stop!" shrieked the poor boy in his agony. "I'll do everything you tell me to, if you won't strike me again!"

This piteous appeal seemed to have no effect upon the cruel man, and he continued to whip the boy, despite his cries and entreaties until his arm fairly ached from the exertion, and Toby's body was crossed and recrossed with the livid marks of the cane.

"Now, let's see whether you'll 'tend to your work or not!" said the man as he flung Toby from him with such force that the boy staggered, reeled, and nearly fell into the little brook that flowed by the roadside.

"I'll make you understand that all the friends you've whined around in this show can't save you from a lickin' when I get ready to give you one! Now go an' do your work that ought to have been done an hour ago!"

Mr. Lord walked away with the proud consciousness of a man who has achieved a great victory, and Toby was limping painfully along toward the cart that was used in conveying Mr. Lord's stock in trade, when he felt a tiny hand slip into his, and heard a childish voice say:

"Don't cry, Toby. Some time, when I get big enough, I'll make Mr. Lord sorry that he whipped you as he did. And I'm big enough now to tell him just what kind of man I think he is."

Looking around, Toby saw his little acquaintance of the evening previous, and he tried to force back the big tears that were rolling down his cheeks as he said in a voice choked with grief, "You're awful good, an' I don't mind the lickin' when you say you're sorry for me. I s'pose I deserve it for runnin' away from Uncle Dan'l."

"Did it hurt you much?" she asked feelingly.

"It did when he was doin' it," replied Toby manfully, "but it don't a bit now that you've come."

"Then I'll go and talk to that Mr. Lord, and I'll come and see you again after we get into town," said the little miss, as she hurried away to tell the candy vendor what she thought of him.

That day, as on all others since he had been with the circus, Toby went to his work with a heavy heart, and time and time again did he count the money which had been given him by kind-hearted strangers, to see whether he had enough to warrant his attempting to run away. Three dollars and twenty-five cents was the total amount of his treasure, and, large as that sum appeared to him, he could not satisfy himself that he had sufficient to enable him to get back to the home which he had so wickedly left. Whenever he thought of his home, of the Uncle Daniel who had in charity cared for him—a motherless, fatherless boy—and of returning to it, with not even as much right as the Prodigal Son, of whom he had heard Uncle Daniel tell, his heart sank within him. And he doubted whether he would be allowed to remain, even if he should be so fortunate as ever to reach Guilford again.

This day passed, so far as Toby was concerned, very much as had the others: he could not satisfy either of his employers, try as hard as he might; but, as usual, he met with two or three kindly disposed people, who added to the fund that he was accumulating for his second venture of running away by the little gifts of money, each one of which gladdened his heart and made his trouble a trifle less hard to bear.

During the entire week he was thus equally fortunate. Each day added something to his fund, and each night it seemed to Toby that he was one day nearer the freedom for which he so ardently longed.

The skeleton, the fat lady, Old Ben, the Albino Children, little Ella, and even the sword swallower all gave him a kindly word as they passed him while he was at his work or saw him as the preparations for the grand entrée were being made.

The time had passed slowly to Toby, and yet Sunday came again—as Sundays always come; and on this day Old Ben hunted him up, made him wash his face and hands until they fairly shone from very cleanliness, and then took him to church. Toby was surprised to find that it was really a pleasant thing to be able to go to church after being deprived of it, and was more light-hearted than he had yet been since he left Guilford when he returned to the tent at noon.

The skeleton had invited him to another dinner party; but Toby had declined the invitation, agreeing to present himself in time for supper instead. He hardly cared to go through the ordeal of another state dinner; and besides, he wanted to go off to the woods with the old monkey, where he could enjoy the silence of the forest, which seemed like a friend to him, because it reminded him of home.

Taking the monkey with him as usual, he inquired the nearest way to a grove, and, without waiting for dinner, started off for an afternoon's quiet enjoyment.

[12]

Toby's Great Misfortune

THE TOWN in which the circus remained over Sunday was a small one, and a brisk walk of ten minutes sufficed to take Toby into a secluded portion of a very thickly grown wood, where he could lie upon the mossy ground and fairly revel in freedom.

As he lay upon his back, his hands under his head and his eyes directed to the branches of the trees above, where the birds twittered and sang, and the squirrels played in fearless sport, the monkey enjoyed himself, in his way, by playing all the monkey antics he knew of. He scrambled from tree to tree, swung himself from one branch to the other by the aid of his tail, and amused both himself and his master, until, tired by his exertions, he crept down by Toby's side and lay there in quiet, restful content.

One of Toby's reasons for wishing to be by himself that afternoon was that he wanted to think over some plan of escape, for he believed that he had nearly money enough to enable him to make a bold stroke for freedom and Uncle Daniel's. Therefore, when the monkey nestled down by his side, he was all ready to confide in him that which had been occupying his busy little brain for the past three days.

"Mr. Stubbs," he announced to the monkey in a very solemn tone, "we're goin' to run away in a day or two."

Mr. Stubbs did not seem to be moved in the least at this very startling piece of intelligence, but winked his bright eyes in unconcern. And Toby, seeming to think that everything which he said had been understood by the monkey, continued: "I've got a good deal of money now, an' I guess there's enough for us to start out on. We'll get away some night an' stay in the woods till they get through hunting for us, an' then we'll go back to Guilford an' tell Uncle Dan'l if he'll only take us back we'll never go to sleep in meetin' any more, an' we'll be just as good as we know how. Now let's see how much money we've got."

Toby drew from a pocket, which he had been at a great deal of trouble to make in his shirt, a small bag of silver and spread it upon the ground, where he could count it at his leisure.

The glittering coin instantly attracted the monkey's attention, and he tried by every means to thrust his little black paw into the pile; but Toby would allow nothing of that sort, and pushed him away quite roughly. Then he grew excited and danced and scolded around Toby's treasure, until the boy had hard work to count it.

He did succeed, however, and as he carefully replaced it in the bag, he said to the monkey, "There's seven dollars an' thirty cents in that bag, an' every cent of it is mine. That ought to take care of us for a good while, Mr. Stubbs; an' by the time we get home we shall be rich men."

The monkey showed his pleasure at this intelligence by putting his hand inside Toby's clothes to find the bag of treasure that he had seen secreted there, and two or three times, to the great delight of both himself and the boy, he drew forth the bag, which was immediately taken away from him.

The shadows were beginning to lengthen in the woods, and, heeding this warning of the coming night, Toby took the monkey on his arm and started for home, or for the tent, which was the only place he could call home.

As he walked along, he tried to talk to his pet in a serious manner, but the monkey, remembering where he had seen the bright coins secreted, tried so hard to get at them that finally Toby lost all patience and gave him quite a hard cuff on the ear, which had the effect of keeping him quiet for a time.

That night Toby took supper with the skeleton and his wife, and he enjoyed the meal, even though it was made from what had been left of the turkey that served as the noonday feast, more than he did the state dinner, where he was obliged to pay for what he ate by the torture of making a speech.

There were no guests but Toby present; and Mr. and Mrs. Treat were not only very kind, but so attentive that he was actually afraid he should eat so much as to stand in need of some of the catnip tea which Mrs. Treat had said she gave to her husband when he had been equally foolish. The skeleton would pile his plate high with turkey bones from one side, and the fat lady would heap it up, whenever she could find a chance, with all sorts of food from the other, until Toby pushed back his chair, his appetite completely satisfied, as if it never had been so before.

Toby had discussed the temper of his employer

with his host and hostess, and, after some considerable conversation, confided in them his determination to run away.

"I'd hate awfully to have you go," said Mrs. Treat reflectively, "but it's a good deal better for you to get away from that Job Lord if you can. It wouldn't do to let him know that you had any idea of goin', for he'd watch you as a cat watches a mouse, an' never let you go so long as he saw a chance to keep you. I heard him tellin' one of the drivers the other day that you sold more goods than any other boy he ever had an' he was going to keep you all summer."

"Be careful in what you do, my boy," said the skeleton sagely, as he arranged a large cushion in an armchair and proceeded to make ready for his after-dinner nap, "be sure that you're all ready before you start, an', when you do go, get a good ways ahead of him; for if he should ever catch you, the trouncin' you'd get would be awful."

Toby assured his friends that he would use every endeavor to make his escape successful when he did start, and Mrs. Treat, with an eye to the boy's comfort, said, "Let me know the night you're goin', an' I'll fix you up something to eat, so's you won't be hungry before you come to a place where you can buy something."

As these kind-hearted people talked with him and were ready thus to aid him in every way that lay in their power, Toby thought that he had been very fortunate in thus having made so many kind friends in a place where he was having so much trouble.

It was not until he heard the sounds of preparation for departure that he left the skeleton's tent, and then, with Mr. Stubbs clasped tightly to his breast, he hurried over to the wagon where Old Ben was nearly ready to start.

"All right, Toby," said the old driver, as the boy came in sight, "I was afraid you was going to keep me waitin' for the first time. Jump right up on the box, for there hain't no time to lose, an' I guess you'll have to carry the monkey in your arms, for I don't want to stop to open the cage now."

"I'd just as soon carry him, an' a little rather," said Toby, as he clambered up on the high seat and arranged a comfortable place in his lap for his pet to sit.

In another moment the heavy team had started, and nearly the entire circus was on the move. "Now tell me what you've been doin' since I left you," said Old Ben, after they were well clear of the town, and he could trust his horses to follow the team ahead. "I s'pose you've been to see the skeleton an' his mountain of a wife?"

Toby gave a clear account of where he had been and what he had done, and when he concluded, he told Old Ben of his determination to run away and asked his advice on the matter.

"My advice," said Ben, after he had waited some time, to give due weight to his words, "is that you clear out from this show just as soon as you can. This hain't no fit place for a boy of your age to be in, an' the sooner you get back where you started from, an' get to school, the better. But Job Lord will do all he can to keep you from goin', if he thinks you have an idea of leavin' him."

Toby assured Ben, as he had assured the skeleton and his wife, that he would be very careful in all he did, and lay his plans with the utmost secrecy; and then he asked whether Ben thought the amount of money which he had would be sufficient to carry him home.

"Waal, that depends," said the driver slowly. "If

you go to spreadin' yourself all over creation, as boys are very apt to do, your money won't go very far; but if you look at your money two or three times afore you spend it, you ought to get back and have a dollar or two left."

The two talked, and Old Ben offered advice, until Toby could hardly keep his eyes open, and almost before the driver concluded his sage remarks, the boy had stretched himself on the top of the wagon, where he had learned to sleep without being shaken off, and was soon in dreamland.

The monkey, nestled down snug in Toby's bosom, did not appear to be as sleepy as was his master, but popped his head in and out from under the coat, as if watching whether the boy was asleep or not.

Toby was awakened by a scratching on his face, as if the monkey was dancing a hornpipe on that portion of his body, and by a shrill, quick chattering, which caused him to assume an upright position instantly.

He was frightened, although he knew not at what, and looked around quickly to discover the cause of the monkey's excitement.

Old Ben was asleep on his box, while the horses jogged along behind the other teams, and Toby failed to see anything whatever which should have caused his pet to become so excited.

"Lie down an' behave yourself," said Toby, as sternly as possible, and as he spoke, he took his pet by the collar, to oblige him to obey his command.

The moment that he did this he saw the monkey throw something out into the road, and the next instant he also saw that he held something tightly clutched in his other paw.

It required some little exertion and active movement on Toby's part to enable him to get hold of that paw, in order to discover what it was which Mr. Stubbs had captured; but the instant he did succeed there went up from his heart such a cry of sorrow as caused Old Ben to start up in alarm, and the monkey to cower and whimper like a whipped dog.

"What is it, Toby? What's the matter?" asked the old driver, as he peered out into the darkness ahead, as if he feared some danger threatened them from that quarter. "I don't see anything. What is it?"

"Mr. Stubbs has thrown all my money away," cried Toby, holding up the almost empty bag, which a short time previous had been so well filled with silver.

"Stubbs—thrown—the—money—away?" repeated Ben, with a pause between each word, as if he could not understand that which he himself was saying.

"Yes," sobbed Toby, as he shook out the remaining contents of the bag, "there's only half a dollar, an' all the rest is gone."

"The rest gone!" again repeated Ben. "But how come the monkey to have the money?"

"He tried to get at it out in the woods, an' I s'pose the moment I got asleep, he felt for it in my pockets. This is all there is left, an' he threw away some just as I woke up."

Again Toby held the bag up where Ben could see it, and again his grief broke out anew.

Ben could say nothing. He realized the whole situation: that the monkey had got at the money bag while Toby was sleeping, that in his play he had thrown it away piece by piece, and he knew that that small amount of silver represented liberty in the boy's eyes. He felt that there was nothing he could say which would assuage Toby's grief and he remained silent.

"Don't you s'pose we could go back an' get it?"

asked the boy, after the intensity of his grief had somewhat subsided.

"No, Toby, it's gone," replied Ben sorrowfully. "You couldn't find it if it was daylight, an' you don't stand a ghost of a chance now in the dark. Don't take on so, my boy. I'll see if we can't make it up to you in some way."

Toby gave no heed to this last remark of Ben's. He hugged the monkey convulsively to his breast, as if he would seek consolation from the very one who had wrought the ruin, and, rocking himself to and fro, he said, in a voice full of tears and sorrow:

"Oh, Mr. Stubbs, why did you do it? Why did you do it? That money would have got us away from this hateful place, an' we'd gone back to Uncle Dan'l's, where we'd have been *so* happy, you an' me. An' now it's all gone—all gone. What made you, Mr. Stubbs—what made you do such a bad, cruel thing? Oh! what made you?"

"Don't, Toby. Don't take on so," said Ben soothingly. "There wasn't so very much money there, after all, an' you'll soon get as much more."

"But it won't be for a good while, an' we could have been in the good old home long before I can get so much again."

"That's true, my boy, but you must kinder brace up an' not give way so about it. Perhaps I can fix it so the fellers will make it up to you. Give Stubbs a good poundin', an' perhaps that'll make you feel better."

"That won't bring back my money, an' I don't want to whip him," cried Toby, hugging his pet the closer because of this suggestion. "I know what it is to get a whippin', an' I wouldn't whip a dog, much less Mr. Stubbs, who didn't know any better."

"Then you must try to take it like a man," said Ben, who could think of no other plan by which the boy might soothe his feelings. "It hain't half so bad as it might be, an' you must try to keep a stiff upper lip, even if it does seem hard at first."

This keeping a stiff upper lip in the face of all the trouble he was having was all very well to talk about, but Toby could not reduce it to practice, or, at least, not so soon after he knew of his loss, and he continued to rock the monkey back and forth, to whisper in his ear now and then, and to cry as if his heart was breaking, for nearly an hour.

Ben tried, in his rough, honest way, to comfort him, but without success, and it was not until the boy's grief had spent itself that he would listen to any reasoning.

All this time the monkey had remained perfectly quiet, submitting to Toby's squeezing without making any effort to get away and behaving as if he knew he had done wrong and was trying to atone for it. He looked up into the boy's face every now and then with such a penitent expression that Toby finally assured him of forgiveness and begged him not to feel so badly.

[13]

Toby Attempts to Resign
His Situation

AT LAST it was possible for Toby to speak of his loss with some degree of calmness, and then he immediately began to reckon up what he could have done with the money if he had not lost it.

"Now see here, Toby," said Ben earnestly, "don't go to doin' anything of that kind. The money's lost, an' you can't get it back by talkin'. So the very best thing for you is to stop thinkin' what you could do if you had it, an' just to look at it as a goner."

"But—" persisted Toby.

"I tell you there's no buts about it," said Ben rather sharply. "Stop talkin' about what's gone, an' just go to thinkin' how you'll get more. Do what you've a mind to the monkey, but don't keep broodin' over what you can't help."

Toby knew that the advice was good, and he struggled manfully to carry it into execution, but it was very hard work. At all events, there was no sleep for his eyes that night, and when, just about daylight, the train halted to wait a more reasonable hour in which to enter the town, the thought of what he might have done with his lost money was still in Toby's mind.

Only once did he speak crossly to the monkey, and that was when he put him into the cage preparatory to commencing his morning's work. Then he said:

"You wouldn't had to go into this place many times more if you hadn't been so wicked, for by tomorrow night we'd been away from this circus an' on the way to home an' Uncle Dan'l. Now you've spoiled my chance an' your own for a good while to come, an' I hope before the day is over, you'll feel as bad about it as I do."

It seemed to Toby as if the monkey understood just what he said to him, for he sneaked over into one corner, away from the other monkeys, and sat there looking very penitent and very dejected.

Then, with a heavy heart, Toby began his day's work.

Hard as had been Toby's lot previous to losing his money and difficult as it had been to bear the cruelty of Mr. Job Lord and his precious partner, Mr. Jacobs, it was doubly hard now while this sorrow was fresh upon him.

Previous to this, when he had been kicked or cursed by one or the other of the partners, Toby thought exultantly that the time was not very far distant when he should be beyond the reach of his brutal taskmasters, and that thought had given him strength to bear all that had been put upon him.

Now the time of his deliverance from this bondage seemed very far off, and each cruel word or blow caused him the greater sorrow, because of the thought that but for the monkey's wickedness he would have been nearly free from that which made his life so very miserable.

If he had looked sad and mournful before, he looked doubly so now, as he went his dreary round of the tent, crying, "Here's your cold lemonade," or "Fresh-baked peanuts, ten cents a quart," and each day there were some in the audience who pitied the boy because of the misery which showed so plainly in his face, and they gave him a few cents more than his price for what he was selling or gave him money without buying anything at all, thereby aiding him to lay up something again toward making his escape.

Those few belonging to the circus who knew of Toby's intention to escape tried their best to console him for the loss of his money, and that kind-hearted couple, the skeleton and his fat wife, tried to force him to take a portion of their scanty earnings in the place of that which the monkey had thrown away. But this Toby positively refused to do, and to the arguments which they advanced as reasons why they should help him along, he only replied that until he could get the money by his own exertions, he would remain with Messrs. Lord and Jacobs and get along as best he could.

Every hour in the day the thought of what might have been if he had not lost his money so haunted his mind that finally he resolved to make one bold stroke and tell Mr. Job Lord that he did not want to travel with the circus any longer.

As yet he had not received the two dollars which had been promised him for his two weeks' work, and another one was nearly due. If he could get this money, it might, with what he had saved again, suffice to pay his railroad fare to Guilford, and if it would not, he resolved to accept from the skeleton sufficient to make up the amount needed.

He naturally shrunk from the task; but the hope

that he might possibly succeed gave him the necessary amount of courage, and when he had gotten his work done on the third morning after he had lost his money and Mr. Lord appeared to be in an unusually good temper, he resolved to try the plan.

It was just before the dinner hour. Trade had been exceptionally good, and Mr. Lord had even spoken in a pleasant tone to Toby when he told him to fill up the lemonade pail with water, so that the stock might not be disposed of too quickly and with too little profit.

Toby poured in quite as much water as he thought the already weak mixture could receive and retain any flavor of lemon; and then, as his employer motioned him to add more, he mixed another quart in, secretly wondering what it would taste like.

"When you're mixin' lemonade for circus trade," said Mr. Lord, in such a benign, fatherly tone that one would have found it difficult to believe that he ever spoke harshly, "don't be afraid of water, for there's where the profit comes in. Always have a piece of lemon peel floatin' on the top of every glass, an' it tastes just as good to people as if it cost twice as much."

Toby could not agree exactly with that opinion, neither did he think it wise to disagree, more especially since he was going to ask the very great favor of being discharged. Therefore he nodded his head gravely and began to stir up what it pleased Mr. Lord to call lemonade, so that the last addition might be more thoroughly mixed with the others.

Two or three times he attempted to ask the favor which seemed a very great one, and each time the words stuck in his throat, until it seemed to him that he should never succeed in getting them out.

Finally, in his despair, he stammered out:

"Don't you think you could find another boy in this town, Mr. Lord?"

Mr. Lord moved round sideways, in order to bring his crooked eye to bear squarely on Toby, and then there was a long interval of silence, during which time the boy's color rapidly came and went and his heart beat very fast with suspense and fear.

"Well, what if I could?" he said at length. "Do you think that trade is so good I could afford to keep two boys, when there isn't half work enough for one?"

Toby stirred the lemonade with renewed activity, as if by this process he was making both it and his courage stronger, and said, in a low voice, which Mr. Lord could scarcely hear:

"I didn't think that; but you see I ought to go home, for Uncle Dan'l will worry about me, an', besides, I don't like a circus very well."

Again there was silence on Mr. Lord's part, and again the crooked eye glowered down on Toby.

"So," he said, and Toby could see that his anger was rising very fast, "you don't like a circus very well an' you begin to think that your Uncle Daniel will worry about you, eh? Well, I want you to understand that it don't make any difference to me whether you like a circus or not, and I don't care how much your Uncle Daniel worries. You mean that you want to get away from me, after I've been to all the trouble and expense of teaching you the business?"

Toby bent his head over the pail, and stirred away as if for dear life.

"If you think you're going to get away from here until you've paid me for all you've eat, an' all the time I've spent on you, you're mistaken, that's all. You've had an easy time with me, too easy, in fact, and that's what ails you. Now, you just let me hear

two words more out of your head about going away,
only two more, an' I'll show you what a whipping is.
I've only been playing with you before when you
thought you was getting a whipping, but you'll find
out what it means if I so much as see a thought in
your eyes about goin' away. An' don't you dare to
try to give me the slip in the night an' run away, for
if you do, I'll follow you an' have you arrested. Now
you mind your eye in the future."

It is impossible to say how much longer Mr. Lord
might have continued this tirade, had not a member
of the company, one of the principal riders, called
him to one side to speak with him.

Poor Toby was so much confused by the angry
words which had followed his very natural and certainly very reasonable suggestion that he paid no
attention to anything around him, until he heard his
own name mentioned. Then, fearing lest some new
misfortune was about to befall him, he listened intently.

"I'm afraid you couldn't do much of anything with
him," he heard Mr. Lord say. "He's had enough of
this kind of life already, so he says, an' I expect the
next thing he does will be try to run away."

"I'll risk his getting away from you, Job," he heard
the other say, "but of course I've got to take my
chances. I'll take him in hand from eleven to twelve
each day, just your slack time of trade, and I'll not
only give you half of what he can earn in the next
two years, but I'll pay you for his time if he gives us
the slip before the season is out."

Toby knew that they were speaking of him, but
what it all meant he could not imagine.

"What are you going to do with him first?" Job
asked.

"Just put him right into the ring and teach him

what riding is. I tell you, Job, the boy's smart enough, and before the season's over I'll have him so that he can do some of the bareback acts, and perhaps we'll get some money out of him before we go into winter quarters."

Toby understood the meaning of their conversation only too well, and he knew that his lot, which before seemed harder than he could bear, was about to be intensified through this Mr. Castle, of whom he had frequently heard, and who was said to be a rival of Mr. Lord's, so far as brutality went. The two men now walked toward the large tent, and Toby was left alone with his thoughts and the two or three little boy customers, who looked at him wonderingly and envied him because he belonged to the circus.

During the ride that night he told Old Ben what he had heard, confidently expecting that that friend at least would console him, but Ben was not the champion which he had expected. The old man who had been with a circus, "man and boy, nigh to forty years," did not seem to think it any calamity that he was to be taught to ride.

"That Mr. Castle is a little rough on boys," Old Ben said thoughtfully, "but it'll be a good thing for you, Toby. Just so long as you stay with Job Lord you won't be nothin' more'n a candy boy; but after you know how to ride, it'll be another thing, an' you can earn a good deal of money, an' be your own boss."

"But I don't want to stay with the circus," whined Toby. "I don't want to learn to ride an' I do want to get back to Uncle Dan'l."

"That may all be true, an' I don't dispute it," said Ben, "but you see, you didn't stay with your Uncle Daniel when you had the chance, an' you did come with the circus. You've told Job you wanted to leave, an' he'll be watchin' you all the time to see that you don't give him the slip. Now, what's the consequence? Why, you can't get away for a while anyhow, an' you'd better try to amount to something while you are here. Perhaps after you've got so you can ride, you may want to stay; an' I'll see to it that you get all of your wages, except enough to pay Castle for learnin' of you."

"I sha'n't want to stay," said Toby. "I wouldn't stay if I could ride all the horses at once, an' was gettin' a hundred dollars a day."

"But you can't ride one horse, an' you hain't gettin' but a dollar a week, an' still I don't see any chance of your gettin' away yet awhile," said Ben, in a matter-of-fact tone, as he devoted his attention again to his horses, leaving Toby to his own reflections and the positive conviction that boys who run away from home do not have a good time, except in stories.

The next forenoon, while Toby was deep in the excitement of selling to a boy no larger than himself and with just as red hair, three cents' worth of peanuts and two sticks of candy, and while the boy was trying to induce him to "throw in" a piece of gum, because of the quantity purchased, Job Lord called him aside, and Toby knew that his troubles had begun.

"I want you to go in an' see Mr. Castle; he's goin' to show you how to ride," said Mr. Lord, in as kindly a tone as if he were conferring some favor on the boy.

If Toby had dared to, he would have rebelled then and there and refused to go, but as he hadn't the courage for such proceeding, he walked meekly into the tent and toward the ring.

[14]

Mr. Castle Teaches Toby
to Ride

WHEN TOBY got within sight of the ring, he was astonished at what he saw. A horse with a broad wooden saddle was being led slowly around the ring. Mr. Castle was standing on one side with a long whip in his hand, and on the tent pole, which stood in the center of the ring, was a long arm, from which dangled a leathern belt attached to a long rope that was carried through the end of the arm and run down to the base of the pole.

Toby knew well enough why the horse, the whip, and the man were there, but the wooden projection from the tent pole, which looked so much like a gallows, he could not understand at all.

"Come now," said Mr. Castle, cracking his whip ominously as Toby came in sight, "why weren't you here before?"

"Mr. Lord just sent me in," said Toby, not expecting that his excuse would be received, for they never had been since he had arrived at the height of his ambition by joining the circus.

"Then I'll make Mr. Job understand that I am to have my full hour of your time, and if I don't get it, there'll be trouble between us."

It would have pleased Toby very well to have had Mr. Castle go out with his long whip just then and make trouble for Mr. Lord, but Mr. Castle had not the time to spare, because of the trouble which he was about to make for Toby, and that he commenced on at once.

"Well, get in here and don't waste any more time," he said sharply.

Toby looked around curiously for a moment, and not understanding exactly what he was expected to get in and do, asked, "What shall I do?"

"Pull off your boots, coat, and vest."

Since there was no other course than to learn to ride, Toby wisely concluded that the best thing he could do would be to obey his new master without question, so be began to take off his clothes with as much alacrity as if learning to ride was the one thing upon which he had long set his heart.

Mr. Castle was evidently accustomed to prompt obedience, for he not only took it as a matter of course but endeavored to hurry Toby in the work of undressing.

With his desire to please and urged by Mr. Castle's words and the ominous shaking of his whip, Toby's preparations were soon made and he stood before his instructor clad only in his shirt, trousers, and stockings.

The horse was led around to where he stood, and when Mr. Castle held out his hand to help him to mount, Toby jumped up quickly without aid, thereby making a good impression at the start as a willing lad.

"Now," said the instructor, as he pulled down the

leathern belt which hung from the rope and fastened it around Toby's waist, "stand up in the saddle and try to keep there. You can't fall, because the rope will hold you up, even if the horse goes out from under you; but it isn't hard work to keep on, if you mind what you are about, and if you don't, this whip will help you. Now stand up."

Toby did as he was bid, and as the horse was led at a walk and as he had the long bridle to aid him in keeping his footing, he had no difficulty in standing during the time that the horse went once around the ring; but that was all.

Mr. Castle seemed to think that this was preparation enough for the boy to be able to understand how to ride and he started the horse into a canter. As might have been expected, Toby lost his balance, the horse went on ahead, and he was left dangling at the end of the rope, very much like a crab that has just been caught by the means of a pole and line.

Toby kicked, waved his hands, and floundered about generally, but all to no purpose, until the horse came around again, and then he made frantic efforts to regain his footing, which efforts were aided, or perhaps it would be more proper to say retarded, by the long lash of Mr. Castle's whip that played around his legs with merciless severity.

"Stand up! Stand up!" cried his instructor, as Toby reeled first to one side and then to the other, now standing erect in the saddle and now dangling at the end of the rope, with the horse almost out from under him.

This command seemed needless, as it was exactly what Toby was trying to do; but as it was given, he struggled all the harder, until it seemed to him that the more he tried the less did he succeed.

And this first lesson progressed in about the same

Toby was left dangling at the end of the rope

way until the hour was over, save that now and then Mr. Castle would give him some good advice, but oftener he would twist the long lash of the whip around the boy's legs with such force that Toby believed the skin had been taken entirely off.

It may have been a relief to Mr. Castle when this first lesson was concluded and it certainly was to Toby, for he had had all the teaching in horsemanship that he wanted, and he thought, with deepest sorrow, that this would be of daily occurrence during all the time he remained with the circus.

As he went out of the tent, he stopped to speak with his friend, the old monkey, and his troubles seemed to have increased when he stood in front of the cage calling, "Mr. Stubbs! Mr. Stubbs!" and the old fellow would not even come down from off the lofty perch where he was engaged in monkey gymnastics with several younger companions. It seemed to him, as he afterward told Ben, "as if Mr. Stubbs had gone back on him because he knew that he was in trouble."

When he went toward the booth, Mr. Lord looked at him around the corner of the canvas, for it seemed to Toby that his employer could look around a square corner with much greater ease than he could straight ahead, with a disagreeable leer in his eye, as if he enjoyed the misery which he knew his little clerk had just undergone.

"Can you ride yet?" he asked mockingly, as Toby stepped behind the counter to attend to his regular line of business.

Toby made no reply, for he knew that the question was only asked sarcastically and not through any desire for information. In a few moments Mr. Lord left him to attend to the booth alone and went into the tent, where Toby rightly conjectured he had gone to question Mr. Castle upon the result of the lesson just given.

That night Old Ben asked him how he had got on while under the teaching of Mr. Castle; and Toby, knowing that the question was asked because of the real interest which Ben had in his welfare, replied:

"If I was tryin' to learn how to swing around the ring, strapped to a rope, I should say that I got along first rate. But I don't know much about the horse, for I was only on his back a little while at a time."

"You'll get over that soon," said Old Ben patronizingly, as he patted him on the back. "You remember my words, now. I say that you've got it in you, an' if you've a mind to take hold an' try to learn, you'll come out on the top of the heap yet an' be one of the smartest riders they've got in this show."

"I don't want to be a rider," said Toby sadly, "I only want to get back home once more, an' then you'll see how much it'll take to get me away again."

"Well," said Ben quietly, "be that as it may, while you're here the best thing you can do is to take hold an' get ahead just as fast as you can. It'll make it a mighty sight easier for you while you're with the show an' it won't spoil any of your chances for runnin' away whenever the time comes."

Toby fully appreciated the truth of this remark, and he assured Ben that he should do all in his power to profit by the instruction given and to please this new master who had been placed over him.

And with this promise he lay back on the seat and went to sleep, not to awaken until the preparations were being made for the entrée into the next town and Mr. Lord's harsh voice had cried out his name, with no gentle tone, several times.

Toby's first lesson with Mr. Castle was the most

pleasant one he had, for after the boy had once been into the ring, his master seemed to expect that he could do everything which he was told to do. And when he failed in any little particular, the long lash of the whip would go curling around legs or arms, until the little fellow's body and limbs were nearly covered with the blue-and-black stripes.

For three lessons only was the wooden upright used to keep him from falling. After that he was forced to ride standing erect on the broad wooden saddle, or pad, as it is properly called, and whenever he lost his balance and fell, there was no question asked as to whether or not he had hurt himself, but he was mercilessly cut with the whip.

Messrs. Lord and Jacobs gained very much by comparison with Mr. Castle in Toby's mind. He had thought that his lot could not be harder than it was with them, but when he had experienced the pains of two or three of Mr. Castle's lessons in horsemanship, he thought that he would stay with the candy vendors all the season cheerfully rather than take six more lessons of Mr. Castle.

Night after night he fell asleep from the sheer exhaustion of crying, as he had been pouring out his woes in the old monkey's ears and laying his plans to run away. Now, more than ever, was he anxious to get away, and yet each day was taking him farther from home and consequently necessitating a larger amount of money with which to start. As Old Ben did not give him as much sympathy as Toby thought he ought to give—for the old man, while he would not allow Mr. Job Lord to strike the boy if he was near, thought it a necessary portion of the education for Mr. Castle to lash him all he had a mind to—he poured out all his troubles in the old monkey's ears and kept him with him from the time he ceased work at night until he was obliged to commence again in the morning.

The skeleton and his wife thought Toby's lot a hard one and tried by every means in their power to cheer the poor boy. Neither one of them could say to Mr. Castle what they had said to Mr. Lord, for the rider was a far different sort of person and one whom they would not be allowed to interfere with in any way. Therefore poor Toby was obliged to bear his troubles and his whippings as best he might, with only the thought to cheer him of the time when he could leave them all by running away.

But, despite all his troubles, Toby learned to ride faster than his teacher had expected he would, and in three weeks he found little or no difficulty in standing erect while his horse went around the ring at his fastest gait. After that had been accomplished, his progress was more rapid and he gave promise of becoming a very good rider—a fact which pleased both Mr. Castle and Mr. Lord very much, as they fancied that in another year Toby would be the source of a very good income to them.

The proprietor of the circus took considerable interest in Toby's instruction and promised Mr. Castle that Mademoiselle Jeannette and Toby should do an act together in the performance just as soon as the latter was sufficiently advanced. The boy's costume had been changed after he could ride without falling off, and now while he was in the ring, he wore the same as that used by the regular performers.

The little girl had, after it was announced that she and Toby were to perform together, been an attentive observer during the hour that Toby was under Mr. Castle's direction, and she gave him many suggestions that were far more valuable and quicker to be acted upon than those given by the teacher himself.

"Tomorrow you two will go through the exercise together," said Mr. Castle to Toby and Ella, at the close of one of Toby's lessons, after he had become so skillful that he could stand with ease on the pad and even advanced so far that he could jump through a hoop without falling more than twice out of three times.

The little girl appeared highly delighted by this information and expressed her joy.

"It will be real nice," she said to Toby after Mr. Castle had left them alone. "I can help you lots, and it won't be very long before we can do an act all by ourselves in the performance and then won't the people clap their hands when we come in!"

"It'll be better for you tomorrow than it will for me," said Toby, rubbing his legs sorrowfully, still feeling the sting of the whip. "You see, Mr. Castle won't dare to whip you, an' he'll make it all count on me, 'cause he knows Mr. Lord likes to have him whip me."

"But I sha'n't make any mistake," said Ella confidently, "and so you won't have to be whipped on my account. And while I am on the horse, you can't be whipped, for he couldn't do it without whipping me, so you see you won't get only half as much."

Toby brightened up a little under the influence of this argument, but his countenance fell again as he thought that his chances of getting away from the circus were growing less each day.

"You see, I want to get back to Uncle Dan'l an' Guilford," he said confidentially, "I don't want to stay here a single minute."

Ella opened her eyes in wide astonishment as she cried, "Don't want to stay here? Why don't you go home, then?"

" 'Cause Job Lord won't let me," said Toby, wondering if it was possible that his little companion did not know exactly what sort of man his master was.

Then he told her, after making her give him all kinds of promises, including the ceremony of crossing her throat, that she would never tell a single soul, that he had had many thoughts and had formed all kinds of plans for running away. He told her about losing his money, about his friendship for the skeleton and the fat lady, and at last he confided in her that he was intending to take the old monkey with him when he should make the attempt.

She listened with the closest attention, and when he told her that his little hoard had now reached the sum of seven dollars and ten cents—almost as much as he had before—she said eagerly, "I've got three little gold dollars in my trunk, an' you shall have them all. They're my very own, for Mamma gave them to me to do just what I wanted to with them. But I don't see how you can take Mr. Stubbs with you, for that would be stealing."

"No, it wouldn't, neither," said Toby stoutly. "Wasn't he give to me to do just as I wanted to with? An' didn't the boss say he was all mine?"

"Oh, I'd forgotten that," said Ella thoughtfully. "I suppose you can take him; but he'll be awfully in the way, won't he?"

"No," said Toby, anxious to say a good word for his pet. "He always does just as I want him to, an' when I tell him what I'm tryin' to do, he'll be as good as anything. But I can't take your dollars."

"Why not?"

" 'Cause that wouldn't be right for a boy to let a girl littler than himself help him. I'll wait till I get money enough of my own, an' then I'll go."

"But I want you to take my money, too; I want you to have it."

"No, I can't take it," said Toby, shaking his head resolutely as he put the golden temptation from him. And then, as a happy thought occurred to him, he said quickly, "I tell you what to do with your dollars: you keep them till you grow up to be a woman, an' when I'm a man, I'll come, an' then we'll buy a circus of our own. I think, perhaps, I'd like to be with a circus if I owned one myself. We'll have lots of money then, an' we can do just what we want to."

This idea seemed to please the little girl, and the two began to lay all sorts of plans for the time when they should be man and woman, have lots of money, and be able to do just as they wanted to.

They had been sitting on the edge of the newly made ring while they were talking, and before they had half finished making plans for the future, one of the attendants came in to put things to order, and they were obliged to leave their seats, she going to the hotel to get ready for the afternoon's performance and Toby to try to do such work as Mr. Job Lord had laid out for him.

Just ten weeks from the time Toby had first joined the circus, Mr. Castle informed him and Ella that they were to appear in public on the following day. They had been practicing daily, and Toby had become so skillful that both Mr. Castle and Mr. Lord saw that the time had come when he could be made to earn some money for them.

[15]

Toby's Friends Present Him with a Costume

DURING THIS time Toby's funds had accumulated rather slower than on the first few days he was in the business, but he had saved eleven dollars, and Mr. Lord had paid him five dollars of his salary, so that he had the, to him, enormous sum of sixteen dollars. And he had about made up his mind to make one effort for liberty, when the news came that he was to ride in public.

He had, in fact, been ready to run away any time within the past week, but, as if they had divined his intentions, both Mr. Castle and Mr. Lord had kept a very strict watch over him, one or the other keeping him in sight from the time he got through with his labors at night until they saw him on the cart with Old Ben.

"I was just gettin' ready to run away," said Toby to Ella, on the day Mr. Castle gave his decision as to their taking part in the performance, and while they were walking out of the tent, "an' I shouldn't wonder now if I got away tonight."

"Oh, Toby!" exclaimed the girl, as she looked reproachfully at him, "after all the work we've had to get ready, you won't go off and leave me before we've had a chance to see what the folks will say when they see us together?"

It was impossible for Toby to feel any delight at the idea of riding in public, and he would have been willing to have taken one of Mr. Lord's most severe whippings if he could have escaped. But he and Ella had become such firm friends and he had conceived such a boyish admiration for her, that he felt as if he were willing to bear almost anything for the sake of giving her pleasure. Therefore he said, after a few moments' reflection, "Well, I won't go tonight, anyway, even if I have the best chance that ever was. I'll stay one day more, anyhow, an' perhaps I'll have to stay a good many."

"That's a nice boy," said Ella positively, as Toby thus gave his decision, "and I'll kiss you for it."

Before Toby fully realized what she was about, almost before he had understood what she said, she had put her arms around his neck and given him a good, sound kiss right on his freckled face.

Toby was surprised, astonished, and just a little bit ashamed. He had never been kissed by a girl before —very seldom by anyone, save the fat lady—and he hardly knew what to do or say. He blushed until his face was almost as red as his hair, and this color had the effect of making his freckles stand out with startling distinctness. Then he looked carefully around to see if anyone had seen them.

"I never had a girl kiss me before," said Toby hesitatingly, "an' you see it made me feel kinder queer to have you do it out here, where everybody could see."

"Well, I kissed you because I like you very much, and because you are going to stay and ride with me tomorrow," she said positively, and then she added, slyly, "I may kiss you again, if you don't get a chance to run away very soon."

"I wish it wasn't for Uncle Dan'l an' the rest of the folks at home, an' there wasn't any such men as Mr. Lord an' Mr. Castle, an' then I don't know but I might want to stay with the circus, 'cause I like you awful much."

And as he spoke, Toby's heart grew very tender toward the only girl friend he had ever known.

By this time they had reached the door of the tent, and as they stepped outside, one of the drivers told them that Mr. Treat and his wife were very anxious to see both of them in their tent.

"I don't believe I can go," said Toby doubtfully, as he glanced toward the booth where Mr. Lord was busy in attending to customers and evidently waiting for Toby to relieve him so that he could go to his dinner, "I don't believe Mr. Lord will let me."

"Go and ask him," said Ella eagerly. "We won't be gone but a minute."

Toby approached his employer with fear and trembling. He had never before asked leave to be away from his work, even for a moment, and he had no doubt but that his request would be refused with blows.

"Mr. Treat wants me to come in his tent for a minute. Can I go?" he asked in a timid voice and in such a low tone as to render it almost inaudible.

Mr. Lord looked at him for an instant, and Toby was sure that he was making up his mind whether to kick him or catch him by the collar and use the rubber cane on him. But he had no such intention evidently, for he said in a voice unusually mild, "Yes, an' you needn't come to work again until it's time to go into the tent."

Toby was almost alarmed at this unusual kindness, and it puzzled him so much that he would have forgotten he had permission to go away if Ella had not pulled him gently by the coat.

If he had heard a conversation between Mr. Lord and Mr. Castle that very morning, he would have understood why it was that Mr. Lord had so suddenly become kind. Mr. Castle had told Job that the boy had really shown himself to be a good rider and that in order to make him more contented with his lot and to keep him from running away, he must be used more kindly and perhaps be taken from the candy business altogether, which latter advice Mr. Lord did not look upon with favor, because of the large sales which the boy made.

When they reached the skeleton's tent, they found to their surprise that no exhibition was being given at that hour, and Ella said, with some concern, "How queer it is that the doors are not open! I do hope that they are not sick."

Toby felt a strange sinking at his heart as the possibility suggested itself that one or both of his kind friends might be ill, for they had both been so kind and attentive to him that he had learned to love them very dearly.

But the fears of both the children were dispelled when they tried to get in at the door and were met by the smiling skeleton himself, who said, as he threw the canvas aside as far as if he were admitting his own enormous Lilly:

"Come in, my friends, come in. I have had the exhibition closed for one hour, in order that I might show my appreciation of my friend, Mr. Tyler."

Toby looked around in some alarm, fearing that Mr. Treat's friendship was about to be displayed in one of his state dinners, which he had learned to fear rather than enjoy. But, as he saw no preparations for dinner, he breathed more freely and wondered what all this ceremony could possibly mean.

Neither he nor Ella was long left in doubt, for as soon as they had entered, Mrs. Treat waddled from behind the screen which served them as a dressing room, with a bundle in her arms, which she handed to her husband.

He took it and, quickly mounting the platform, leaving Ella and Toby below, he commenced to speak with very many flourishes of his thin arms.

"My friends," he began, as he looked down upon his audience of three, who were listening in the following attitudes: Ella and Toby were standing upon the ground at the foot of the platform, looking up with wide-open, staring eyes. His fleshy wife was seated on a bench which had evidently been placed in such a position below the speaker's stand that she could hear and see all that was going on without the fatigue of standing up, which, for one of her size, was really very hard work. "My friends," repeated the skeleton, as he held his bundle in front of him with one hand and gesticulated with the other, "we all of us know that tomorrow our esteemed and worthy friend, Mr. Toby Tyler, makes his first appearance in any ring, and we all of us believe that he will soon become a bright and shining light in the profession which he is so soon to enter."

The speaker was here interrupted by loud applause from his wife, and he profited by the opportunity to wipe a stray drop of perspiration from his fleshless face. Then, as the fat lady ceased the exertion of clapping her hands, he continued:

"Knowing that our friend, Mr. Tyler, was being instructed, preparatory to dazzling the public with his talents, my wife and I began to prepare for him some slight testimonial of our esteem. And, being informed by Mr. Castle some days ago of the day on which he was to make his first appearance before the public, we were enabled to complete our little gift in time for the great and important event."

Here the skeleton paused to take a breath, and Toby began to grow most uncomfortably red in the face. Such praise made him feel very awkward.

"I hold in this bundle," continued Mr. Treat as he waved the package on high, "a costume for our bold and worthy equestrian and a sash to match for his beautiful and accomplished companion. In presenting these little tokens, my wife, who has embroidered every inch of the velvet herself, and I feel proud to know that, when the great and auspicious occasion occurs tomorrow, the worthy Mr. Tyler will step into the ring in a costume which we have prepared expressly for him. Thus, when he does himself honor by his performance and earns the applause of the multitude, he will be doing honor and earning applause for the work of our hands—my wife Lilly and myself. Take them, my boy, and when you array yourself in them tomorrow, you will remember that the only Living Skeleton and the wonder of the nineteenth century in the shape of the Mammoth Lady, are present in their works if not in their persons."

As he finished speaking, Mr. Treat handed the bundle to Toby and then joined in the applause which was being given by Mrs. Treat and Ella.

Toby unrolled the package and found that it contained a circus rider's costume of pink tights and blue velvet trunks, collar and cuffs, embroidered in white and plentifully spangled with silver. In addition was a wide blue sash for Ella, embroidered to correspond with Toby's costume.

The little fellow was both delighted with the gift and at a loss to know what to say in response. He looked at the costume over and over again, and the tears of gratitude that these friends should have been so good to him came into his eyes. He saw, however, that they were expecting him to say something in reply and, laying the gift on the platform, he said to the skeleton and his wife:

"You've been so good to me ever since I've been with the circus that I wish I was big enough to say somethin' more than that I'm much obliged, but I can't. One of these days, when I'm a man, I'll show you how much I like you, an' then you won't be sorry that you was good to such a poor little runaway boy as I am."

Here the skeleton broke in with such loud applause and so many cries of "Hear! hear!" that Toby grew still more confused and forgot entirely what he was intending to say next.

"I want you to know how much obliged I am," he said, after some hesitation, "an' when I wear 'em, I'll ride just the best I know how, even if I don't want to, an' you shan't be sorry that you gave them to me."

As Toby concluded, he made a funny little awkward bow and then seemed to be trying to hide himself behind a chair from the applause which was given so generously.

"Bless your dear little heart!" said the fat lady, after the confusion had somewhat subsided. "I know you will do your best, anyway, and I'm glad to know that you're going to make your first appearance in something that Samuel and I made for you."

Ella was quite as well pleased with her sash as

Toby was with his costume and thanked Mr. and Mrs. Treat in a pretty little way that made Toby wish he could say anything half so nicely.

The hour which the skeleton had devoted for the purpose of the presentation and accompanying speeches having elapsed, it was necessary that Ella and Toby should go, and that the doors of the exhibition be opened at once, in order to give any of the public an opportunity of seeing what the placards announced as two of the greatest curiosities on the face of the globe.

That day, while Toby performed his arduous labors, his heart was very light, for the evidences which the skeleton and his wife had given of their regard for him were very gratifying. He determined that he would do his very best to please as long as he was with the circus, and then, when he got a chance to run away, he would do so, but not until he had said good-by to Mr. and Mrs. Treat and thanked them again for their interest in him.

When he had finished his work in the tent that night, Mr. Lord said to him as he patted him on the back in the most fatherly fashion and as if he had never spoken a harsh word to him, "You can't come in here to sell candy now that you are one of the performers, my boy; an' if I can find another boy tomorrow, you won't have to work in the booth any longer. An' your salary of a dollar a week will go on just the same, even if you don't have anything to do but to ride."

This was a bit of news that was as welcome to Toby as it was unexpected, and he felt more happy then than he had for the ten weeks that he had been traveling under Mr. Lord's cruel mastership.

But there was one thing that night that rather damped his joy and that was that he noticed that

Mr. Lord was unusually careful to watch him, not even allowing him to go outside the tent without following. He saw at once that, if he was to have a more easy time, his chances for running away were greatly diminished, and no number of beautiful costumes would have made him content to stay with the circus one moment longer than was absolutely necessary.

That night he told Old Ben of the events of the day and expressed the hope that he might acquit himself creditably when he made his first appearance on the following day.

Ben sat thoughtfully for some time and then, making all the preparations which Toby knew so well signified a long bit of advice, he said, "Toby, my boy, I've been with a circus, man an' boy, nigh to forty years, an' I've seen lots of youngsters start in just as you're goin' to start in tomorrow; but the most of them petered out because they got to knowin' more'n them that learned 'em did. Now, you remember what I say, an' you'll find it good advice. Whatever business you get into, don't think you know all about it before you've begun. Remember that you can always learn somethin', no matter how old you are, an' keep your eyes an' ears open an' your tongue between your teeth, an' you'll amount to somethin', or my name hain't Ben."

[16]

Toby's First Appearance
in the Ring

WHEN THE circus entered the town which had been selected as the place where Toby was to make his début as a circus rider the boy noticed a new poster among the many glaring and gaudy bills which set forth the varied and numerous attractions that were to be found under one canvas for a trifling admission fee, and he noticed it with some degree of interest, not thinking for a moment that it had any reference to him.

"Look there!" said Toby to Ben, as he pointed out the poster, which was printed in very large letters, with gorgeous coloring and surmounted by a picture of two very small people performing all kinds of impossible feats on horseback. "They've got someone else to ride with Ella today. I wonder who it can be?"

Ben looked at Toby for a moment, as if to assure himself that the boy was in earnest in asking the question, and then he relapsed into the worst fit of silent laughing that Toby had ever seen. After he had quite recovered, he asked, "Don't you know who Monsieur Ajax is? Hain't you never seen him?"

"No," replied Toby, at a loss to understand what there was so very funny in this very natural question. "I thought that I was goin' to ride with Ella."

"Why, that's you!" almost screamed Ben in delight. "Monsieur Ajax means you, didn't you know it? You don't suppose they would go to put 'Toby Tyler' on the bills, do you? How it would look! 'Mademoiselle Jeannette an' Monsieur Toby Tyler!' "

Ben was off in one of his laughing spells again, and Toby sat there, stiff and straight, hardly know-

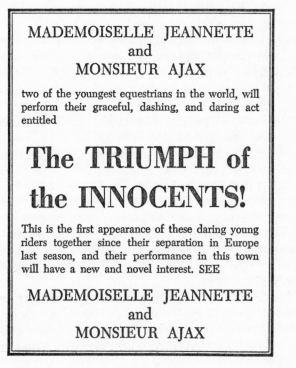

MADEMOISELLE JEANNETTE
and
MONSIEUR AJAX

two of the youngest equestrians in the world, will perform their graceful, dashing, and daring act entitled

The TRIUMPH of the INNOCENTS!

This is the first appearance of these daring young riders together since their separation in Europe last season, and their performance in this town will have a new and novel interest. SEE

MADEMOISELLE JEANNETTE
and
MONSIEUR AJAX

ing whether to join in the mirth or to get angry at the sport which had been made of his name.

"I don't care," he said at length. "I'm sure I think Toby Tyler sounds just as well as Monsieur Ajax, an' I'm sure it fits me a good deal better."

"That may be," said Ben soothingly, "but you see it wouldn't go down so well with the public. They want furrin riders, an' they must have 'em, even if it does spoil your name."

Despite the fact that he did not like the new name that had been given him, Toby could not but feel pleased at the glowing terms in which his performance was set off, but he did not at all relish the lie that was told about his having been with Ella in Europe, and he would have been very much better pleased if that portion of it had been left off.

During the forenoon he did not go near Mr. Lord nor his candy stand, for Mr. Castle kept him and Ella busily engaged in practicing the feat which they were to perform in the afternoon, and it was almost time for the performance to begin before they were allowed even to go to their dinner.

Ella, who had performed several years, was very much more excited over the coming début than Toby was, and the reason why he did not show more interest was probably because of his great desire to leave the circus as soon as possible. And during that forenoon he thought very much more of how he should get back to Guilford and Uncle Daniel than he did of how he should get along when he stood before the audience.

Mr. Castle assisted his pupil to dress, and when that was done to his entire satisfaction, he said, in a stern voice, "Now, you can do this act all right, and if you slip up on it and don't do it as you ought to, I'll give you such a whipping when you come out of the ring that you'll think Job was only fooling with you when he tried to whip you."

Toby had been feeling reasonably cheerful before this, but these words dispelled all his cheerful thoughts and he was looking most disconsolate when Old Ben came into the dressing tent.

"All ready are you, my boy?" said the old man in his cheeriest voice. "Well, that's good, an' you look as nice as possible. Now remember what I told you last night, Toby, an' go in there to do your level best an' make a name for yourself. Come out here with me an' wait for the young lady."

These cheering words of Ben's did Toby as much good as Mr. Castle's had the reverse, and as he stepped out of the dressing room to the place where the horses were being saddled, Toby resolved that he would do his very best that afternoon, if for no other reason than to please his old friend.

Toby was not naturally what might be called a pretty boy, for his short red hair and his freckled face prevented any great display of beauty, but he was a good, honest-looking boy, and in his tasteful costume looked very nice indeed—so nice that, could Mrs. Treat have seen him just then, she would have been very proud of her handiwork and hugged him harder than ever.

He had been waiting but a few moments when Ella came from her dressing room, and Toby was very much pleased when he saw by the expression of her face that she was perfectly satisfied with his appearance.

"We'll both do just as well as we can," she whispered to him, "and I know the people will like us and make us come back after we get through. And if they do, Mamma says she'll give each one of us a gold dollar."

She had taken hold of Toby's hand as she spoke, and her manner was so earnest and anxious that Toby was more excited than he ever had been about his début; and, had he gone into the ring just at that moment, the chances are that he would have surprised even his teacher by his riding.

"I'll do just as well as I can," said Toby, in reply to his little companion, "an' if we earn the dollars, I'll have a hole bored in mine, an' you shall wear it around your neck to remember me by."

"I'll remember you without that," she whispered, "and I'll give you mine, so that you shall have so much the more when you go to your home."

There was no time for further conversation, for Mr. Castle entered just then to tell them that they must go in in another moment. The horses were all ready—a black one for Toby and a white one for Ella—and they stood champing their bits and pawing the earth in their impatience until the silver bells with which they were decorated rang out quick, nervous little chimes that accorded very well with Toby's feelings.

Ella squeezed Toby's hand as they stood waiting for the curtain to be raised that they might enter, and he had just time to return it when the signal was given, and almost before he was aware of it, they were standing in the ring, kissing their hands to the crowds that packed the enormous tent to its utmost capacity.

Thanks to the false announcement about the separation of the children in Europe and their reunion in this particular town, the applause was long and loud, and before it had died away, Toby had time to recover a little from the queer feeling which this sea of heads gave him.

He had never seen such a crowd before, except as

he had seen them as he walked around at the foot of the seats, and then they had simply looked like so many human beings. But as he saw them now from the ring, they appeared like strange rows of heads without bodies, and he had hard work to keep from running back behind the curtain whence he had come.

Mr. Castle acted as the ringmaster this time, and after he had introduced them, very much after the fashion of the posters, and the clown had repeated some funny joke, the horses were led in, and they were assisted to mount.

"Don't mind the people at all," said Mr. Castle, in a low voice, "but ride just as if you were alone here with me."

The music struck up, the horses cantered around the ring, and Toby had really started as a circus rider.

"Remember," said Ella to him in a low tone, just as the horses started, "you told me that you would ride just as well as you could, and we must earn the dollars Mamma promised."

It seemed to Toby at first as if he could not stand up; but by the time they had ridden around the ring once and Ella had again cautioned him against making any mistake, for the sake of the money which they were going to earn, he was calm and collected enough to carry out his part of the "act" as well as if he had been simply taking a lesson.

The act consisted in their riding side by side, jumping over banners and through hoops covered with paper, and then the most difficult portion began.

The saddles were taken off the horses, and they were to ride first on one horse and then on the other, until they concluded their performance by riding twice around the ring side by side, standing on their horses, each one with a hand on the other's shoulder.

All this was successfully accomplished without a single error, and when they rode out of the ring, the applause was so great as to leave no doubt but that they would be recalled and thus earn the promised money.

In fact, they had hardly got inside the curtain when one of the attendants called to them, and before they had time even to speak to each other, they were in the ring again, repeating the last portion of their act.

When they came out of the ring for the second time, they found Old Ben, the skeleton, the fat lady, and Mr. Job Lord waiting to welcome them. But before anyone could say a word, Ella had stood on tiptoe again and given Toby just such another kiss as she did when he told her that he would surely stay long enough to appear in the ring with her once.

"That's because you rode so well and helped me so much," she said, as she saw Toby's cheeks growing a fiery red, and then she turned to those who were waiting to greet her.

Mrs. Treat took her in her enormous arms and having kissed her, put her down quickly and clasped Toby as if he had been a very small walnut and her arms a very large pair of nutcrackers.

"Bless the boy!" she exclaimed, as she kissed him again and again with an energy and force that made her kisses sound like the crack of the whip, and caused the horses to stamp in affright. "I knew he'd amount to something one of these days, an' Samuel an' I had to come out, when business was dull, just to see how he got along."

It was some time before she would unloose him from her motherly embrace, and when she did, the

They rode standing on their horses

skeleton grasped him by the hand and said, in the most pompous and affected manner:

"Mr. Tyler, we're proud of you, and when we saw that costume of yours that my Lilly embroidered with her own hands, we was both proud of it and what it contained. You're a great rider, my boy, a great rider, and you'll stand at the head of the profession some day, if you only stick to it."

"Thank you, sir," was all Toby had time to say before Old Ben had him by the hand, and the skeleton was pouring out his congratulations in little Miss Ella's ear.

"Toby, my boy, you did well, an' now you'll amount to something, if you only remember what I told you last night," said Ben, as he looked upon the boy whom he had come to think of as his protégé, with pride. "I never seen anybody of your age do any better. An' now, instead of bein' only a candy peddler, you're one of the stars of the show."

"Thank you, Ben," was all that Toby could say, for he knew that his old friend meant every word that he said, and it pleased him so much that he could say no more than "Thank you" in reply.

"I feel as if your triumph was mine," said Mr. Lord, looking benignly at Toby from out his crooked eye and assuming the most fatherly tone at his command. "I have learned to look upon you almost as my own son, and your success is very gratifying to me."

Toby was not at all flattered by this last praise. If he had never seen Mr. Lord before, he might, and probably would, have been deceived by his words, but he had seen him too often and under too many painful circumstances to be at all swindled by his words.

Toby was very much pleased with his success and

by the praise he received from all, and when the proprietor of the circus came along, patted him on the head and told him that he rode very nicely, he was quite happy, until he chanced to see the greedy twinkle in Mr. Lord's eye. Then he knew that all this success and all this praise were only binding him faster to the show which he was so anxious to escape from; his pleasure vanished very quickly, and in its stead came a bitter, homesick feeling which no amount of praise could banish.

It was Old Ben who helped him to undress after the skeleton and the fat lady had gone back to their tent, and Ella had gone to dress for her appearance with her mother, for now she was obliged to ride twice at each performance. When Toby was in his ordinary clothes again, Ben said:

"Now that you're one of the performers, Toby, you won't have to sell candy any more, an' you'll have the most of your time to yourself, so let's you an' I go out an' see the town."

"Don't you s'pose Mr. Lord expects me to go to work for him again today?"

"An' s'posin' he does?" said Ben with a chuckle. "You don't s'pose the boss would let anyone that rides in the ring stand behind Job Lord's counter, do you? You can do just as you have a mind to, my boy, an' I say to you, let's go out an' see the town. What do you say to it?"

"I'd like to go first-rate, if I dared to," replied Toby, thinking of the many whippings he had received for far less than that which Ben now proposed he should do.

"Oh, I'll take care that Job don't bother you, so come along," and Ben started out of the tent and Toby followed, feeling considerably frightened at this first act of disobedience against his old master.

[17]

Off for Home

DURING THIS walk Toby learned many things that were of importance to him, so far as his plan for running away was concerned. In the first place, he gleaned from the railroad posters that were stuck up in the hotel to which they went that he could buy a ticket for Guilford for seven dollars, and also that, by going back to the town from which they had just come, he could go to Guilford by steamer for five dollars.

By returning to this last town, and Toby calculated that the fare on the stage back there could not be more than a dollar, he would have ten dollars left, and that surely ought to be sufficient to buy food enough for two days for the most hungry boy that ever lived.

When they returned to the circus grounds, the performance was over, and Mr. Lord was in the midst of the brisk trade which he usually had after the afternoon performance; and yet, so far from scolding

Toby for going away, he actually smiled and bowed at him as he saw him go by with Ben.

"See there, Toby," said the old driver to the boy, as he gave him a vigorous poke in the ribs and then went off into one of his dreadful laughing spells, "see what it is to be a performer an' not workin' for such an old fossil as Job is! He'll be so sweet to you now that sugar won't melt in his mouth, an' there's no chance of his ever attemptin' to whip you again."

Toby made no reply, for he was too busily engaged thinking of something which had just come into his mind to know that his friend had spoken.

But as Old Ben hardly knew whether the boy had answered him or not, owing to his being obliged to struggle with his breath lest he should lose it in the second laughing spell that attacked him, the boy's thoughtfulness was not particularly noticed.

Toby walked around the show grounds for a little while with his old friend, and then the two went to supper, where Toby performed quite as great wonders in the way of eating as he had in the afternoon by riding.

As soon as the supper was over, he quietly slipped away from Old Ben, and at once paid a visit to Mr. and Mrs. Treat, whom he found cozily engaged with their supper behind the screen.

They welcomed Toby most cordially, and, despite his assertions that he had just finished a very hearty meal, the fat lady made him sit down to the box which served as table, and insisted on his trying some of her doughnuts.

Under all these pressing attentions it was some time before Toby found a chance to say that which he had come to say, and when he did, he was almost at a loss how to proceed. But at last he commenced by starting abruptly on his subject with the words:

"I've made up my mind to leave tonight."

"Leave tonight?" repeated the skeleton inquiringly, not for a moment believing that Toby could think of running away after the brilliant success he had just made. "What do you mean, Toby?"

"Why, you know that I've been wantin' to get away from the circus," said Toby, a little impatient that his friend should be so wonderfully stupid, "an' I think that I'll have as good a chance now as ever I shall, so I'm goin' to try it."

"Bless us!" exclaimed the fat lady, in a gasping way. "You don't mean to say that you're goin' off just when you've started in the business so well? I thought you'd want to stay after you'd been so well received this afternoon."

"No," said Toby, and one quick little sob popped right up from his heart and out before he was aware of it. "I learned to ride because I had to, but I never give up runnin' away. I must see Uncle Dan'l an' tell him how sorry I am for what I did; an' if he won't have anything to say to me, then I'll come back, but if he'll let me, I'll stay there, an' I'll be *so* good that by-'n'-by he'll forget that I run off and left him without sayin' a word."

There was such a touch of sorrow in his tones, so much pathos in his way of speaking, that good Mrs. Treat's heart was touched at once, and putting her arms around the little fellow as if to shield him from some harm, she said tenderly, "And so you shall go, Toby, my boy. But if you ever want a home or anybody to love you, come right here to us, and you'll never be sorry. So long as Sam keeps thin and I fat enough to draw the public, you never need say that you're homeless, for nothing would please us better than to have you come to live with us."

For reply Toby raised his head and kissed her on the cheek, a proceeding which caused her to squeeze him harder than ever.

During this conversation the skeleton had remained very thoughtful. After a moment or two he got up from his seat, went outside the tent, and presently returned with a quantity of silver ten-cent pieces in his hand.

"Here, Toby," he said, and it was to be seen that he was really too much affected even to attempt one of his speeches, "it's right that you should go, for I've known what it is to feel just as you do. What Lilly said about your having a home with us I say, an' here's five dollars that I want you to take to help you along."

At first Toby stoutly refused to take the money, but they both insisted to such a degree that he was actually forced to, and then he stood up to go.

"I'm goin' to try to slip off after Job packs up the outside booth if I can," he said, "an' it was to say good-by that I come around here."

Again Mrs. Treat took the boy in her arms, as if it were one of her own children who was leaving her, and as she stroked his hair back from his forehead, she said, "Don't forget us, Toby, even if you never do see us again. Try an' remember how much we cared for you an' how much comfort you're taking away from us when you go; for it was a comfort to see you around, even if you wasn't with us very much. Don't forget us, Toby, an' if you ever get the chance, come an' see us. Good-by, Toby, good-by." And the kind-hearted woman kissed him again and again and then turned her back resolutely upon him, lest it should be bad luck to him if she again saw him after saying good-by.

The skeleton's parting was not quite so demonstrative. He clasped Toby's hand with one set of his fleshless fingers, while with the other he wiped one or two suspicious-looking drops of moisture from his eyes, as he said, "I hope you'll get along all right, my boy, and I believe you will. You will get home to Uncle Daniel and be happier than ever, for now you know what it is to be entirely without a home. Be a good boy, mind your uncle, go to school, and one of these days you'll make a good man. Good-by, my boy."

The tears were now streaming down Toby's face very rapidly. He had not known, in his anxiety to get home, how very much he cared for this strangely assorted couple, and now it made him feel very miserable and wretched that he was going to leave them. He tried to say something more, but the tears choked his utterance and he left the tent quickly to prevent himself from breaking down entirely.

In order that his grief might not be noticed and the cause of it suspected, Toby went out behind the tent and, sitting there on a stone, he gave way to the tears which he could no longer control.

While he was thus engaged, heeding nothing which passed around him, he was startled by a cheery voice which cried, "Halloo! Down in the dumps again? What is the matter now, my bold equestrian?"

Looking up, he saw Ben standing before him, and he wiped his eyes hastily, for here was another from whom he must part and to whom a good-by must be spoken.

Looking around to make sure that no one was within hearing, he went up very close to the old driver, and said, in almost a whisper, "I was feelin' bad 'cause I just come from Mr. and Mrs. Treat, an'

I've been sayin' good-by to them. I'm goin' to run away tonight."

Ben looked at him for a moment, as if he doubted whether the boy knew exactly what he was talking about, and then said, "So you still want to go home, do you?"

"Oh, yes, Ben, *so* much," was the reply, in a tone which expressed how dear to him was the thought of being in his old home once more.

"All right, my boy. I won't say one word agin it, though it do seem too bad, after you've turned out to be such a good rider," said the old man thoughtfully. "It's better for you, I know, for a circus hain't no place for a boy, even if he wants to stay, an' I can't say but I'm glad you're still determined to go."

Toby felt relieved at the tone of this leave-taking. He had feared that Old Ben, who thought a circus rider was almost on the topmost round of Fortune's ladder, would have urged him to stay, since he had made his début in the ring, and he was almost afraid that he might take some steps to prevent his going.

"I wanted to say good-by now," said Toby, in a choking voice, "'cause perhaps I shan't see you again."

"Good-by, my boy," said Ben as he took the boy's hand in his. "Don't forget this experience you've had in runnin' away. An' if ever the time comes that you feel as if you wanted to know that you had a friend, think of Old Ben, an' remember that his heart beats just as warm for you as if he was your father. Good-by, my boy, good-by, an' may the good God bless you!"

"Good-by, Ben," said Toby, and then, as the old driver turned and walked away, wiping something from his eye with the cuff of his sleeve, Toby gave full vent to his tears and wondered why it was that he was such a miserable little wretch.

There was one more good-by to be said and that Toby dreaded more than all the others. It was to Ella. He knew that she would feel badly to have him go, because she liked to ride the act with him that gave them such applause, and he felt certain that she would urge him to stay.

Just then the thought of another of his friends, one who had not yet been warned of what very important matter was to occur, came into his mind, and he hastened toward the old monkey's cage. His pet was busily engaged in playing with some of the younger members of his family and for some moments could not be induced to come to the bars of the cage.

At last, however, Toby did succeed in coaxing him forward and then, taking him by the paw and drawing him as near as possible, Toby whispered, "We're goin' to run away tonight, Mr. Stubbs, an' I want you to be all ready to go the minute I come for you."

The old monkey winked both eyes violently and then showed his teeth to such an extent that Toby thought he was laughing at the prospect, and he said, a little severely, "If you had as many friends as I have got in this circus you wouldn't laugh when you was goin' to leave them. Of course I've got to go, an' I want to go; but it makes me feel bad to leave the skeleton an' the fat woman an' Old Ben an' little Ella. But I mustn't stand here. You be ready when I come for you, an' by mornin' we'll be so far off that Mr. Lord nor Mr. Castle can't catch us."

The old monkey went toward his companions, as if he were in high glee at the trip before him, and

Toby went into the dressing tent to prepare for the evening's performance, which was about to commence.

It appeared to the boy as if everyone was unusually kind to him that night, and, feeling sad at leaving those in the circus who had befriended him, Toby was unusually attentive to everyone around him. He ran on some trifling errand for one, helped another in his dressing, and in a dozen kind ways seemed as if trying to atone for leaving them secretly.

When the time came for him to go into the ring and he met Ella, bright and happy at the thought of riding with him and repeating her triumphs of the afternoon, nothing save the thought of how wicked he had been to run away from good old Uncle Daniel and a desire to right that wrong in some way, prevented him from giving up his plan of going back.

The little girl observed his sadness, and she whispered, "Has anyone been whipping you, Toby?"

Toby shook his head. He had thought that he would tell her what he was about to do just before they went into the ring, but her kind words seemed to make that impossible. And he had said nothing, when the blare of the trumpets, the noisy demonstrations of the audience, and the announcement of the clown that the wonderful children riders were now about to appear, ushered them into the ring.

If Toby had performed well in the afternoon, he accomplished wonders on this evening, and they were called back into the ring, not once, but twice, and when finally they were allowed to retire, everyone behind the curtain overwhelmed them with praise.

Ella was so profuse with her kind words, her admiration for what Toby had done, and so delighted at the idea that they were to ride together, that even then the boy could not tell her what he was going to do, but went into his dressing room, resolving that he would tell her all when they both had finished dressing.

Toby made as small a parcel as possible of the costume which Mr. and Mrs. Treat had given him, for he determined that he would take it with him, and, putting it under his coat, went out to wait for Ella. As she did not come out as soon as he expected, he asked someone to tell her that he wanted to see her, and he thought to himself that when she did come she would be in a hurry and could not stop long enough to make any very lengthy objections to his leaving.

But she did not come at all—her mother sent out word that Toby could not see her until after the performance was over, owing to the fact that it was now nearly time for her to go into the ring and she was not dressed yet.

Toby was terribly disappointed. He knew that it would not be safe for him to wait until the close of the performance if he were intending to run away that night, and he felt that he could not go until he had said a few last words to her.

He was in a great perplexity, until the thought came to him that he could write a good-by to her, and by this means any unpleasant discussion would be avoided.

After some little difficulty he procured a small piece of not very clean paper and a very short bit of lead pencil, and using the top of one of the wagons as he sat on the seat for a desk, he indited the following epistle:

deaR ella I Am goin to Run away two night,
& i want two say good by to yu & your mother.
i am Small & unkle Danil says i dont mount two
much, but i am old enuf two know that you have
bin good two me, & when i Am a man i will buy
you a whole cirkus, and we Will ride together.
dont forgit me & I wont yu in haste

TOBY TYLER

Toby had no envelope in which to seal this precious letter, but he felt that it would not be seen by
prying eyes and would safely reach its destination,
if he intrusted it to Old Ben.

It did not take him many moments to find the old
driver, and he said, as he handed him the letter, "I
didn't see Ella to tell her I was goin', so I wrote this
letter, an' I want to know if you will give it to her?"

"Of course I will. But see here, Toby," and Ben
caught him by the sleeve and led him aside where
he would not be overheard, "have you got money
enough to take you home? For if you haven't, I can
let you have some." And Ben plunged his hand into
his capacious pocket, as if he was about to withdraw
from there the entire United States Treasury.

Toby assured him that he had sufficient for all
his wants; but the old man would not be satisfied
until he had seen for himself and then, taking Toby's
hand again, he said, "Now, my boy, it won't do for
you to stay around here any longer. Buy something
to eat before you start an' go into the woods for a
day or two before you take the train or steamboat.
You're too big a prize for Job or Castle to let you go
without a word, an' they'll try their level best to
find you. Be careful, now, for if they should catch
you, good-by any more chances to get away. There,"
and here Ben suddenly lifted him high from the

ground and kissed him, "now get away as fast as you can."

Toby pressed the old man's hand affectionately, and then, without trusting himself to speak, walked swiftly out toward the entrance.

He resolved to take Ben's advice and go into the woods for a short time, and therefore he must buy some provisions before he started.

As he passed the monkey's cage, he saw his pet sitting near the bars and he stopped long enough to whisper, "I'll be back in ten minutes, Mr. Stubbs, an' you be all ready then."

Then he went on, and just as he got near the entrance one of the men told him that Mrs. Treat wished to see him.

Toby could hardly afford to spare the time just then, but he would probably have obeyed the summons if he had known that by so doing he would be caught, and he ran as fast as his little legs would carry him toward the skeleton's tent.

The exhibition was open, and both the skeleton and his wife were on the platform when Toby entered; but he crept around at the back and up behind Mrs. Treat's chair, telling her as he did so that he had just received her message and that he must hurry right back, for every moment was important then to him.

"I put up a nice lunch for you," she said as she kissed him, "and you'll find it on top of the biggest trunk. Now go, and if my wishes are of any good to you, you will get to your Uncle Daniel's house without any trouble. Good-by again, little one."

Toby did not dare to trust himself any longer where everyone was so kind to him. He slipped down from the platform as quickly as possible, found the bundle—and a good-sized one it was too—without any difficulty, and went back to the monkeys' cage.

As orders had been given by the proprietor of the circus that the boy should do as he had a mind to with the monkey, he called Mr. Stubbs, and as he was in the custom of taking him with him at night, no one thought that it was anything strange that he should take him from the cage now.

Mr. Lord or Mr. Castle might possibly have thought it queer had either of them seen the two bundles which Toby carried, but, fortunately for the boy's scheme, they both believed that he was in the dressing tent and consequently thought that he was perfectly safe.

Toby's hand shook so that he could hardly undo the fastening of the cage, and when he attempted to call the monkey to him, his voice sounded so strange and husky that it startled him.

The old monkey seemed to prefer sleeping with Toby rather than with those of his kind in the cage; and as the boy took him with him almost every night, he came on this particular occasion as soon as Toby called, regardless of the strange sound of his master's voice.

With his bundles under his arm and the monkey on his shoulder, with both paws tightly clasped around his neck, Toby made his way out of the tent with beating heart and bated breath.

Neither Mr. Lord, Castle, nor Jacobs was in sight, and everything seemed favorable for his flight. During the afternoon he had carefully noted the direction of the woods, and he started swiftly toward them now, stopping only long enough, as he was well clear of the tents, to say, in a whisper:

"Good-by, Mr. Treat, an' Mrs. Treat, an' Ella, an' Ben. Sometime, when I'm a man, I'll come back an' bring you lots of nice things an' I'll never forget you

—never. When I have a chance to be good to some little boy that felt as bad as I did, I'll do it, an' tell him that it was you did it. Good-by."

Then, turning around, he ran toward the woods as swiftly as if his escape had been discovered and the entire company were in pursuit.

[18]

A Day of Freedom

Toby ran at the top of his speed over the rough road, and the monkey, jolted from one side to the other, clutched his paws more tightly around the boy's neck, looking around into his face as if to ask what was the meaning of this very singular proceeding.

When he was so very nearly breathless as to be able to run no more but was forced to walk, Toby looked behind him and there he could see the bright lights of the circus and hear the strains of the music as he had heard them on the night when he was getting ready to run away from Uncle Daniel. Those very sounds, which reminded him forcibly of how ungrateful he had been to the old man who had cared for him when there was no one else in the world who would do so, made it more easy for him to leave those behind who had been so kind to him when he stood so much in need of kindness.

"We are goin' home, Mr. Stubbs!" he said exultantly to the monkey, "home to Uncle Dan'l an' the boys. An' won't you have a good time when we get there! You can run all over the barn an' up in the trees an' do just what you want to, an' there'll be plenty of fellows to play with you. You don't know half how good a place Guilford is, Mr. Stubbs."

The monkey chattered away as if he were anticipating lots of fun on his arrival at Toby's home, and the boy chattered back, his spirits rising at every step which took him farther away from the collection of tents where he had spent so many wretched hours.

A brisk walk of half an hour sufficed to take Toby to the woods, and after some little search he found a thick clump of bushes in which he concluded he could sleep without the risk of being seen by anyone who might pass that way before he should be awake in the morning.

He had not much choice in the way of a bed, for it was so dark in the woods that it was impossible to collect moss or leaves to make a soft resting place, and the few leaves and pine boughs which he did gather made his place for sleeping but very little softer.

But during the ten weeks that Toby had been with the circus his bed had seldom been anything softer than the seat of the wagon, and it troubled him very little that he was to sleep with nothing but a few leaves between himself and the earth.

Using the bundle in which was his riding costume for a pillow and placing the lunch Mrs. Treat had given him near by, where the monkey could not get at it conveniently, he cuddled Mr. Stubbs up in his bosom and lay down to sleep.

"Mr. Lord won't wake us up in the mornin' an' swear at us for not washin' the tumblers," said Toby in a tone of satisfaction to the monkey, "an' we won't

have to go into the tent tomorrow an' sell sick lemonade an' poor peanuts. But," and here his tone
changed to one of sorrow, "there'll be some there
that'll be sorry not to see us in the mornin', Mr.
Stubbs, though they'll be glad to know that we got
away all right. But won't Mr. Lord swear, an' won't
Mr. Castle crack his whip, when they come to look
round for us in the mornin' and find that we hain't
there!"

The only reply which the monkey made to this
was to nestle his head closer under Toby's coat and
to show, in the most decided manner, that he was
ready to go to sleep.

And Toby was quite as ready to go to sleep as he
was. He had worked hard that day, but the excitement of escaping had prevented him from realizing
his fatigue until after he had lain down. And almost
before he had got through congratulating himself
upon the ease with which he had gotten free, both
he and the monkey were as sound asleep as if they
had been tucked up in the softest bed that was ever
made.

Toby's very weariness was a friend to him that
night, for it prevented him from waking, which, if
he had done so, might have been unpleasant when
he fully realized that he was all alone in the forest,
and the sounds that are always heard in the woods
might have frightened him just the least bit.

The sun was shining directly in his face when Toby
awoke on the following morning, and the old monkey was still snugly nestled under his coat. He sat up
rather dazed at first and then, as he fully realized
that he was actually free from all that had made his
life such a sad and hard one for so many weeks, he
shouted aloud, reveling in his freedom.

The monkey, awakened by Toby's cries, started from his sleep in affright and jumped into the nearest tree, only to chatter, jump, and swing from the boughs when he saw that there was nothing very unusual going on, save that he and Toby were out in the woods again, where they could have no end of a good time and do just as they liked.

After a few moments spent in a short jubilee at their escape, Toby took the monkey on his shoulder and the bundles under his arm again and went cautiously out to the edge of the thicket, where he could form some idea as to whether or not they were pursued.

He had entered the woods at the brow of a small hill when he had fled so hastily on the previous evening and looking down, he could see the spot whereon the tents of the circus had been pitched, but not a sign of them was now visible. He could see a number of people walking around, and he fancied that they looked up ever now and then to where he stood concealed by the foilage.

This gave him no little uneasiness, for he feared that Mr. Lord or Mr. Castle might be among the number and he believed that they would begin a search for him at once, and that the spot where their attention would first be drawn was exactly where he was then standing.

"This won't do, Mr. Stubbs," he said, as he pushed the monkey higher up on his shoulder and started into the thickest part of the woods, "we must get out of this place, an' go farther down, where we can hide till tomorrow mornin'. Besides, we must find some water where we can wash our faces."

The old monkey would hardly have been troubled if they had not had their faces washed for the next

He could see a number of people walking around

month to come, but he grinned and talked as Toby trudged along, attempting to catch hold of the leaves as they were passed and in various other ways impeding his master's progress, until Toby was obliged to give him a most severe scolding in order to make him behave himself in anything like a decent manner.

At last, after fully half an hour's rapid walking, Toby found just the place he wanted in which to pass the time he concluded it would be necessary to spend before he dare venture out to start for home.

It was a little valley entirely filled by trees, which grew so thickly, save in one little spot, as to make it almost impossible to walk through. The one clear spot was not more than ten feet square, but it was just at the edge of a swiftly running brook, and a more beautiful or convenient place for a boy and a monkey to stop who had no tent, nor means to build one, could not well be imagined.

Toby's first act was to wash his face, and he tried to make the monkey do the same, but Mr. Stubbs had no idea of doing any such foolish thing. He would come down close to the edge of the water and look in, but the moment that Toby tried to make him go in, he would rush back among the trees, climb out on some slender bough, and then swing himself down by the tail and chatter away as if making sport of his young master for thinking that he would be so foolish as to soil his face with water.

After Toby had made his toilet, he unfastened the bundle which the fat lady had given him, for the purpose of having breakfast. As much of an eater as Toby was, he could not but be surprised at the quantity of food which Mrs. Treat called a lunch. There were two whole pies and half of another, as many as two dozen doughnuts, several large pieces of cheese, six sandwiches, with a plentiful amount of meat, half a dozen biscuits, nicely buttered, and a large piece of cake.

The monkey had come down from the tree as soon as he saw Toby untying the bundle, and there was quite as much pleasure depicted on his face when he saw the good things that were spread out before him, as there was on Toby's. And he showed his thankfulness at Mrs. Treat's foresight by suddenly snatching one of the doughnuts and running with it up the tree where he knew Toby could not follow.

"Now look here, Mr. Stubbs!" said Toby sternly, "you can have all you want to eat, but you must take it in a decent way, an' not go to cuttin' up any such shines as that."

And after giving this command—which, by the way, was obeyed just about as well as it was understood—Toby devoted his time to his breakfast and he reduced the amount of eatables very considerably before he had finished.

Toby cleared off his table by gathering the food together and putting it back into the paper as well as possible, and then he sat down to think over the situation, and to decide what he had better do.

He felt rather nervous about venturing out when it was possible for Mr. Lord or Mr. Castle to get hold of him again, and as the weather was yet warm during the night, his camping place everything that could be desired, and the stock of food likely to hold out, he concluded that he had better remain there for two days at least. Then he would be reasonably sure that if either of the men whom he so dreaded to see had remained behind for the purpose of catching him, he would have got tired out and gone on.

This point decided upon, the next was to try to fix up something soft for a bed. He had his pocket knife with him, and in his little valley were pine and hemlock trees in abundance. From the tips of their branches he knew that he could make a bed as soft and fragrant as any that could be thought of, and he set to work at once, while Mr. Stubbs continued his antics above his head.

After about two hours' steady work he had cut enough of the tender branches to make himself a bed into which he and the monkey could burrow and sleep as comfortably as if they were in the softest bed in Uncle Daniel's house.

When Toby first began to cut the boughs, he had an idea that he might possibly make some sort of hut, but the two hours' work had blistered his hands, and he was perfectly ready to sit down and rest, without the slightest desire for any other kind of hut than that formed by the trees themselves.

Toby imagined that in that beautiful place he could, with the monkey, stay contented for any number of days, but after he had rested a time, played with his pet a little, and eaten just a trifle more of the lunch, the time passed so slowly that he soon made up his mind to run the risk of meeting Mr. Lord or Mr. Castle again by going out of the woods the first thing the next morning.

Very many times before the sun set that day, was Toby tempted to run the risk that night, for the sake of the change, if no more, but as he thought the matter over, he saw how dangerous such a course would be and he forced himself to wait.

That night he did not sleep as soundly as on the previous one, for the very good reason that he was not as tired. He awoke several times, and the noise of the night birds alarmed him to such an extent that he was obliged to awaken the old monkey for company.

But the night passed despite his fears, as all nights will, whether a boy is out in the woods alone or tucked up in his own little bed at home. In the morning Toby made all possible haste to get away, for each moment that he stayed now made him more impatient to be moving toward home.

He washed himself as quickly as possible, ate his breakfast with the most unseemly haste, and, taking up his bundles and the monkey, once more started, as he supposed, in the direction from which he had entered the woods.

Toby walked briskly along, in the best possible spirits, for his running away was now an accomplished fact and he was going toward Uncle Daniel and home just as fast as possible. He sang "Old Hundred" through five or six times by way of showing his happiness. It is quite likely that he would have sung something a little more lively had he known anything else, but "Old Hundred" was the extent of his musical education, and he kept repeating that, which was quite as satisfactory as if he had been able to go through with every opera that was ever written.

The monkey would jump from his shoulder into the branches above, run along on the trees for a short distance, and then wait until Toby came along, when he would drop down on his shoulder suddenly, and in every other way of displaying monkey delight he showed that he was just as happy as was possible.

Toby trudged on in this contented way for nearly an hour, and every moment expected to step out to the edge of the woods, where he could see houses and men once more. But instead of doing so the forest seemed to grow more dense, and nothing betokened his approach to the village. There was a great fear came into Toby's heart just then, and for a moment he halted in helpless perplexity. His lips began to quiver, his face grew white, and his hand trembled so that the old monkey took hold of one of his fingers and looked at it wonderingly.

[19]

Mr. Stubbs' Mischief
and His Sad Fate

TOBY HAD begun to realize that he was lost in the
woods, and the thought was sufficient to cause
alarm in the mind of one much older than the boy.
He said to himself that he would keep on in the
direction he was then traveling for fifteen minutes;
and as he had no means of computing time, he sat
down on a log, took out the bit of pencil with which
he had written the letter to Ella, and multiplied
sixty by fifteen. He knew that there were sixty seconds to the minute and that he could ordinarily
count one to each second; therefore, when he learned
there were nine hundred seconds in fifteen minutes,
he resolved to walk as straight ahead as possible
until he should have counted that number.

He walked on, counting as regularly as he could,
and thought to himself that he never before realized
how long fifteen minutes were. It really seemed to
him that an hour had passed before he finished
counting, and then when he stopped, there were

no more signs that he was near a clearing than there had been before.

"Ah, Mr. Stubbs, we're lost! We're lost!" he cried, as he laid his cheek on the monkey's head and gave way to the lonesome grief that came over him. "What shall we do? Perhaps we won't ever find our way out, but will die here, an' then Uncle Dan'l won't ever know how sorry I was that I run away."

Then Toby lay right down on the ground and cried so hard that the monkey acted as if it were frightened and tried to turn the boy's face over, and finally leaned down and licked Toby's ear.

This little act, which seemed so much like a kiss, caused Toby to feel no small amount of comfort, and he sat up again, took the monkey in his arms, and began seriously to discuss some definite plan of action.

"It won't do to keep on the way we've been goin', Mr. Stubbs," said Toby, as he looked full in his pet's face—and the old monkey sat as still and looked as grave as it was possible for him to look and sit— "for we must be goin' into the woods deeper. Let's start off this way," and Toby pointed at right angles with the course they had been pursuing, "an' keep right on that way till we come to something or till we drop right down an' die."

It is fair to presume that the old monkey agreed to Toby's plan, for although he said nothing in favor of it he certainly made no objections to it, which to Toby was the same as if his companion had assented to it in the plainest English.

Both the bundles and the monkey were rather a heavy load for a small boy like Toby to carry. But he clung manfully to them, walked resolutely on, without looking to the right or to the left, glad when the old monkey would take a run among the trees, for then he would be relieved of his weight; and glad when he returned, for then he had his company, and that repaid him for any labor which he might have to perform.

Toby was in a hard plight as it was, but without the old monkey for a companion he would have thought his condition was a hundred times worse and would hardly have had the courage to go on as he was going.

On and on he walked, until it seemed to him that he could really go no farther, and yet he could see no signs which indicated the end of the woods. At last he sank upon the ground, too tired to walk another step, saying to the monkey, who was looking as if he would like to know the reason of this pause, "It's no use, Mr. Stubbs, I've got to sit down here an' rest awhile, anyhow. Besides, I'm awfully hungry."

Then Toby commenced to eat his dinner and to give the monkey his, until the thought came to him that he neither had any water nor did he know where to find it, and then, of course, he immediately became so thirsty that it was impossible for him to eat any more.

"We can't stand this," moaned Toby to the monkey. "We've got to have something to drink or else we can't eat all these sweet things, an' I'm so tired that I can't go any farther. Don't let's eat dinner now, but let's stay here an' rest an' then we can keep on an' look for water.'

Toby's resting spell was a long one, for as soon as he stretched himself out on the ground, he was asleep from actual exhaustion and he did not awaken until the sun was just setting. Then he saw that, hard as his troubles had been before, they were about to become, or in fact had become, worse.

He had paid no attention to his bundles when he lay down, and when he awoke, he was puzzled to make out what it was that was strewn around the ground so thickly.

He had looked at it but a very short time when he saw that it was what had been the lunch he had carried so far. After having had the sad experience of losing his money, he understood very readily that the old monkey had taken the lunch while he slept and had amused himself by picking it apart into the smallest particles possible, and then strewn them around on the ground where he now saw them.

Toby looked at them in almost speechless surprise and then he turned to where the old monkey lay, apparently asleep, but as the boy watched him intently, he could see that the cunning animal was really watching him out of one half-closed eye.

"Now you have killed us, Mr. Stubbs," wailed Toby. "We never can find our way out of here. An' now we hain't got anything to eat and by tomorrow we shall be starved to death. Oh dear! Wasn't you bad enough when you threw all the money away, so you had to go an' do this just when we was in awful trouble?"

Mr. Stubbs now looked up as if he had just been awakened by Toby's grief, looked around him leisurely as if to see what could be the matter, and then, apparently seeing for the first time the crumbs that were lying around on the ground, took up some and examined them intently.

"Now don't go to makin' believe that you don't know how they come there," said Toby, showing anger toward his pet for the first time. "You know it was you who did it, for there wasn't anyone else here, an' you can't fool me by lookin' so surprised."

It seemed as if the monkey had come to the conclusion that his little plan of ignorance wasn't the most perfect success, for he walked meekly toward his young master, climbed up on his shoulder, and sat there kissing his ear, or looking down into his eyes, until the boy could resist the mute appeal no longer, but took him into his arms and hugged him closely as he said:

"It can't be helped now, I s'pose, an' we shall have to get along the best way we can, but it was awful wicked of you, Mr. Stubbs, an' I don't know what we're going to do for something to eat."

While the destructive fit was on him, the old monkey had not spared the smallest bit of food but had picked everything into such minute shreds that none of it could be gathered up, and everything was surely wasted.

While Toby sat bemoaning his fate and trying to make out what was to be done for food, the darkness, which had just begun to gather when he first awoke, now commenced to settle around, and he was obliged to seek for some convenient place in which to spend the night before it became so dark as to make the search impossible.

Owing to the fact that he had slept nearly the entire afternoon and also rendered wakeful by the loss he had just sustained, Toby lay awake on the hard ground, with the monkey on his arm, hour after hour, until all kinds of fancies came to him. And in every sound he feared he heard someone from the circus coming to capture him or some wild beast intent on picking his bones.

The cold sweat of fear stood out on his brow, and he hardly dared to breathe, much more to speak, lest the sound of his voice should betray his whereabouts and thus bring his enemies down upon him. The minutes seemed like hours and the hours like days, as he lay there, listening fearfully to every one of the night sounds of the forest. And it seemed to him that he had been there very many hours when at last he fell asleep, and was thus freed from his fears.

Bright and early on the following morning Toby was awake, and as he came to a realizing sense of all the dangers and trouble that surrounded him, he was disposed to give way again to his sorrow, but he said resolutely to himself, "It might be a good deal worse than it is, an' Mr. Stubbs an' I can get along one day without anything to eat. An' perhaps by night we shall be out of the woods, an' then what we get will taste good to us."

He began his walk—which possibly might not end that day—manfully, and his courage was rewarded by soon reaching a number of bushes that were literally loaded down with blackberries. From these he made a hearty meal, and the old monkey fairly reveled in them, for he ate all he possibly could and then stowed away enough in his cheeks to make a good-sized luncheon when he should be hungry again.

Refreshed very much by his breakfast of fruit, Toby again started on his journey with renewed vigor, and the world began to look very bright to him. He had not thought that he might find berries when the thoughts of starvation came into his mind, and now that his hunger was satisfied, he began to believe that he might possibly be able to live, perhaps for weeks, in the woods solely upon what he might find growing there.

Shortly after he had had breakfast, he came upon a brook, which he thought was the same upon whose banks he had encamped the first night he spent in the woods, and, pulling off his clothes, he waded into the deepest part and had a most refreshing bath, although the water was rather cold.

Not having any towels with which to dry himself, he was obliged to sit in the sun until the moisture had been dried from his skin and he could put his clothes on once more. Then he started out on his walk again, feeling that sooner or later he would come out all right.

All this time he had been traveling without any guide to tell him whether he was going straight ahead or around in a circle, and he now concluded to follow the course of the brook, believing that that would lead him out of the forest some time.

During the forenoon he walked steadily, but not so fast that he would get exhausted quickly, and when by the position of the sun he judged that it was noon, he lay down on a mossy bank to rest.

He was beginning to feel sad again. He had found no more berries, and the elation which had been caused by his breakfast and his bath was quickly passing away. The old monkey was in a tree almost directly above his head, stretched out on one of the limbs in the most contented manner possible. As Toby watched him and thought of all the trouble he had caused by wasting the food, thoughts of starvation again came into his mind, and he believed that he should not live to see Uncle Daniel again.

Just when he was feeling the most sad and lonely, and when thoughts of death from starvation were most vivid in his mind, he heard the barking of a dog, which sounded close at hand.

His first thought was that at last he was saved, and he was just starting to his feet to shout for help, when he heard the sharp report of a gun and an

[171]

agonizing cry from the branches above. And the old monkey fell to the ground with a thud that told he had received his death wound.

All this had taken place so quickly that Toby did not at first comprehend the extent of the misfortune which had overtaken him; but a groan from the poor monkey, as he placed one little brown paw to his breast from which the blood was flowing freely and looked up into his master's face with a most piteous expression, showed the poor little boy what a great trouble it was which had now come.

Poor Toby uttered a loud cry of agony, which could not have been more full of anguish had he received the ball in his own breast. And, flinging himself by the side of the dying monkey, he gathered him close to his breast, regardless of the blood that poured over him, and stroking tenderly the little head that had nestled so often in his bosom, said, over and over again, as the monkey uttered short moans of agony, "Who could have been so cruel? Who could have been so cruel?"

Toby's tears ran like rain down his face, and he kissed his dying pet again and again, as if he would take all the pain to himself.

"Oh, if you could only speak to me!" he cried, as he took one of the poor monkey's paws in his hand, and, finding that it was growing cold with the chill of death, put it on his neck to warm it. "How I love you, Mr. Stubbs! An' now you're goin' to die an' leave me! Oh, if I hadn't spoken cross to you yesterday, an' if I hadn't a'most choked you the day that we went to the skeleton's to dinner! Forgive me for ever bein' bad to you, won't you, Mr. Stubbs?"

As the monkey's groans increased in number but diminished in force, Toby ran to the brook, filled his hands with water, and held it to the poor animal's mouth.

He lapped the water quickly and looked up with a human look of gratitude in his eyes, as if thanking his master for that much relief. Then Toby tried to wash the blood from his breast, but it flowed quite as fast as he could wash it away, and he ceased his efforts in that direction and paid every attention to making his friend and pet more comfortable. He took off his jacket and laid it on the ground for the monkey to lie upon. He picked a quantity of large green leaves as a cooling rest for his head and then sat by his side, holding his paws and talking to him with the most tender words his lips, quivering with sorrow as they were, could fashion.

[20]

Home and Uncle Daniel

MEANWHILE THE author of all this misery had come upon the scene. He was a young man, whose rifle and well-filled game bag showed that he had been hunting, and his face expressed the liveliest sorrow for what he had so unwittingly done.

"I didn't know I was firing at your pet," he said to Toby as he laid his hand on his shoulder and endeavored to make him look up. "I only saw a little patch of fur through the trees and, thinking it was some wild animal, I fired. Forgive me, won't you, and let me put the poor brute out of his misery?"

Toby looked up fiercely at the murderer of his pet and asked savagely, "Why don't you go away? Don't you see that you have killed Mr. Stubbs, an' you'll be hung for murder?"

"I wouldn't have done it under any circumstances," said the young man, pitying Toby's grief most sincerely. "Come away, and let me put the poor thing out of its agony."

"How can you do it?" asked Toby bitterly. "He's dying already."

"I know it, and it will be a kindness to put a bullet through his head."

If Toby had been big enough, perhaps there might really have been a murder committed, for he looked up at the man who so coolly proposed to kill the poor monkey after he had already received his death wound that the young man stepped back quickly, as if really afraid that in his desperation the boy might do him some injury.

"Go 'way off," said Toby passionately, "an' don't ever come here again. You've killed all I ever had in this world of my own to love me, an' I hate you. I hate you!"

Then, turning again to the monkey, he put his hands on each side of his head and, leaning down, kissed the little brown lips as tenderly as a mother would kiss her child.

The monkey was growing more and more feeble, and when Toby had shown this act of affection, he reached up his tiny paws, grasped Toby's finger, half raised himself from the ground and then with a convulsive struggle fell back dead, while the tiny fingers slowly relaxed their hold of the boy's hand.

Toby feared that it was death and yet hoped that he was mistaken. He looked into the half open, fast glazing eyes, put his hand over his heart, to learn if it were still beating and getting no responsive look from the dead eyes, feeling no heart throbs from under that gory breast, he knew that his pet was really dead, and he flung himself by his side in all the childish abandonment of grief.

He called the monkey by name, implored him to look at him, and finally bewailed that he had ever left the circus, where at least his pet's life was safe, even if his own back received its daily flogging.

The young man, who stood a silent spectator of

this painful scene, understood everything from Toby's mourning. He knew that a boy had run away from the circus, for Messrs. Lord and Castle had stayed behind one day, in the hope of capturing the fugitive, and they had told their own version of Toby's flight.

For nearly an hour Toby lay by the dead monkey's side, crying as if his heart would break, and the young man waited until his grief should have somewhat exhausted itself and then approached the boy again.

"Won't you believe that I didn't mean to do this cruel thing?" he asked in a kindly voice. "And won't you believe that I would do anything in my power to bring your pet back to life?"

Toby looked at him a moment earnestly and then said slowly, "Yes, I'll try to."

"Now will you come with me, and let me talk to you? For I know who you are and why you are here."

"How do you know that?"

"Two men stayed behind after the circus had left, and they hunted everywhere for you."

"I wish they had caught me," moaned Toby. "I wish they had caught me, for then Mr. Stubbs wouldn't be here dead."

And Toby's grief broke out afresh as he again looked at the poor little stiff form that had been a source of so much comfort and joy to him.

"Try not to think of that now, but think of yourself and of what you will do," said the man soothingly, anxious to divert Toby's mind as much as possible.

"I don't want to think of myself and I don't care what I'll do," sobbed the boy passionately.

"But you must. You can't stay here always, and I

will try to help you to get home, or wherever it is you want to go, if you will tell me all about it."

It was some time before Toby could be persuaded to speak or think of anything but the death of his pet, but the young man finally succeeded in drawing his story from him and then tried to induce him to leave that place and accompany him to the town.

"I can't leave Mr. Stubbs," said the boy firmly. "He never left me the night I got thrown out of the wagon an' he thought I was hurt."

Then came another struggle to induce him to bury his pet. And finally Toby, after realizing the fact that he could not carry a dead monkey with him, agreed to it, but he would not allow the young man to help him in any way or even to touch the monkey's body.

He dug a grave under a little fir tree near by and lined it with wild flowers and leaves, and even then hesitated to cover the body with the earth. At last he bethought himself of the fanciful costume which the skeleton and his wife had given him, and in this he carefully wrapped his dead pet. He had not one regret at leaving the bespangled suit, for it was the best he could command, and surely nothing could be too good for Mr. Stubbs.

Tenderly he laid him in the little grave and, covering the body with flowers, said, pausing a moment before he covered it over with earth, and while his voice was choked with emotion, "Good-by, Mr. Stubbs, good-by! I wish it had been me instead of you that died, for I'm an awful sorry little boy now that you're dead!"

Even after the grave had been filled and a little mound made over it, the young man had the greatest difficulty to persuade Toby to go with him. And when the boy did consent to go at last, he walked very slowly away and kept turning his head to look back just so long as the little grave could be seen.

Then, when the trees shut it completely out from sight, the tears commenced again to roll down Toby's cheeks and he sobbed out, "I wish I hadn't left him. Oh, why didn't I make him lie down by me? An' then he'd be alive now, an' how glad he'd be to know that we was getting out of the woods at last!"

But the man who had caused Toby this sorrow talked to him about other matters, thus taking his mind from the monkey's death as much as possible, and by the time the boy reached the village, he had told his story exactly as it was, without casting any reproaches on Mr. Lord, and giving himself the full share of censure for leaving his home as he did.

Mr. Lord and Mr. Castle had remained in the town but one day, for they were told that a boy had taken the night train that passed through the town about two hours after Toby had escaped, and they had set off at once to act on that information.

Therefore Toby need have no fears of meeting either of them just then and he could start on his homeward journey in peace.

The young man who had caused the monkey's death tried first to persuade Toby to remain a day or two with him and, failing in that, he did all he could toward getting the boy home as quickly and safely as possible. He insisted on paying for his ticket on the steamboat, although Toby did all he could to prevent him, and he even accompanied Toby to the next town, where he was to take the steamer.

He had not only paid for Toby's ticket, but he had paid for a stateroom for him. And when the boy said that he could sleep anywhere and that there was no need of such expense, the man replied, "Those men who were hunting for you have gone down the river and will be very likely to search the boat, when they discover that they started on the wrong scent. They will never suspect that you have got a stateroom, and if you are careful to remain in it during the trip, you will get through safely."

Then when the time came for the steamer to start, the young man said to Toby, "Now, my boy, you won't feel hard at me for shooting the monkey, will you? I would have done anything to have brought him to life, but, as I could not do that, helping you to get home was the next best thing I could do."

"I know you didn't mean to shoot Mr. Stubbs," said Toby, with moistening eyes as he spoke of his pet, "an' I'm sorry I said what I did to you in the woods."

Before there was time to say any more, the warning whistle was sounded, the plank pulled in, the great wheels commenced to revolve, and Toby was really on his way to Uncle Daniel and Guilford.

It was then but five o'clock in the afternoon, and he could not expect to reach home until two or three o'clock in the afternoon of the next day, but he was in a tremor of excitement as he thought that he should walk through the streets of Guilford once more, see all the boys, and go home to Uncle Daniel.

And yet, whenever he thought of that home, of meeting those boys, of going once more to all those old familiar places, the memory of all that he had planned when he should take the monkey with him would come into his mind and damp even his joy, great as it was.

That night he had considerable difficulty in falling asleep, but did finally succeed in doing so. And when he awoke, the steamer was going up the river whose waters seemed like an old friend, because

[179]

"I know you didn't mean to shoot Mr. Stubbs,"
said Toby

they had flowed right down past Guilford on their way to the sea.

At each town where a landing was made Toby looked eagerly out on the pier, thinking that by chance someone from his home might be there and he would see a familiar face again. But all this time he heeded the advice given him and remained in his room, where he could see and not be seen. And it was well for him that he did so, for at one of the landings he saw both Mr. Lord and Mr. Castle come on board the boat.

Toby's heart beat fast and furious, and he expected every moment to hear them at the door demanding admittance, for it seemed to him that they must know exactly where he was secreted.

But no such misfortune occurred. The men had evidently only boarded the boat to search for the boy, for they landed again before the steamer started, and Toby had the satisfaction of seeing their backs as they walked away from the pier. It was some time before he recovered from the fright which the sight of them gave him, but when he did, his thoughts and hopes far outstripped the steamer which, it seemed, was going so slowly, and he longed to see Guilford with an impatience that could hardly be restrained.

At last he could see the spire of the little church on the hill, and when the steamer rounded the point, affording a full view of the town, and sounded her whistle as a signal for those on the shore to come to the pier, Toby could hardly restrain himself from jumping up and down and shouting in his delight.

He was at the gangplank ready to land fully five minutes before the steamer was anywhere near the wharf, and when he recognized the first face on the pier, what a happy boy he was!

He was at home! The dream of the past ten weeks was at length realized and neither Mr. Lord nor Mr. Castle had any terrors for him now.

He ran down the gangplank before it was ready and clasped every boy he saw there round the neck and would have kissed them, if they had shown an inclination to let him do so.

Of course he was overwhelmed with questions, but before he would answer any, he asked for Uncle Daniel and the others at home.

Some of the boys ventured to predict that Toby would get a jolly good whipping for running away, and the only reply which the happy Toby made to that was:

"I hope I will, an' then I'll feel as if I had kinder paid for runnin' away. If Uncle Dan'l will only let me stay with him again, he may whip me every mornin', an' I won't open my mouth to holler."

The boys were impatient to hear the story of Toby's travels, but he refused to tell it them, saying:

"I'll go home, an' if Uncle Dan'l forgives me for bein' so wicked I'll sit down this afternoon an' tell you all you want to know about the circus."

Then, far more rapidly than he had run away from it, Toby ran toward the home which he had called his ever since he could remember, and his heart was full almost to bursting as he thought that perhaps he would be told that he had forfeited all claim to it and that he could never more call it "home" again.

When he entered the old familiar sitting room, Uncle Daniel was seated near the window, alone, looking out wistfully, as Toby thought, across the fields of yellow, waving grain.

Toby crept softly in and, going up to the old man,

knelt down and said very humbly and with his whole soul in the words, "Oh, Uncle Dan'l! If you'll only forgive me for bein' so wicked an' runnin' away an' let me stay here again—for it's all the home I ever had—I'll do everything you tell me to an' never whisper in meetin' or do anything bad."

And then he waited for the words which would seal his fate. They were not long in coming.

"My poor boy," said Uncle Daniel softly, as he stroked Toby's refractory red hair, "my love for you was greater than I knew, and when you left me, I cried aloud to the Lord as if it had been my own flesh and blood that had gone afar from me. Stay here, Toby, my son, and help to support this poor old body as it goes down into the dark valley of the shadow of death, and then, in the bright light of that glorious future, Uncle Daniel will wait to go with you into the presence of Him who is ever a father to the fatherless."

And in Uncle Daniel's kindly care we may safely leave Toby Tyler.